Christmas Crazy in July

CHRISTMAS ONLY COMES ONCE A YEAR

JENNA HENDRICKS

Contents

Chapter 1

Millie

Seriously? Why has everyone gone Christmas Crazy? It's like I've left Earth and stepped into a television show. These women are nuts, and not in a cute and funny way. If I don't get out of here, *I'm* gonna go crazy. But my form of crazy will most likely get me locked in a padded room with a not-so-stylish jacket that ties my arms around my body.

I swear, if I ever meet that celebrity who suggested the entire world celebrate Christmas in July, I'm gonna strangle her! All it took was one post by Gina Montana and the world went wacko. The rest of Hollywood, and even Bollywood, got on the bandwagon and began tweeting and posting all over social media that what the world needs is love—in the form of a jolly old man who flies around the world in one night delivering presents down chimneys.

It didn't matter that Santa normally wears a super-warm fur suit and that reindeer prefer the cold, not the one-hundred-degree weather that so many states, and other countries, experience on July twenty-fifth. Even if they fly at night and it's a lot colder in the air, I know for a fact that Las Vegas is still almost one hundred degrees at night during the height of summer. What sort of jolly can Santa and his eight unlucky reindeer feel in sweltering heat?

Before you go all Christmas Crazy on me too, I know that the Southern Hemisphere celebrates Christmas in their summer each December, so theoretically Santa already knows what it's like to fly in the summer. As do his reindeer. But come on, who in their right mind wants to pretend that Christmas in July is the same as a December Christmas?

It doesn't matter that the entire world missed out on Christmas last December thanks to a world-wide pandemic that closed everything down. We could wait for this December to celebrate as usual. Maybe even buy a few more presents, add a few more lights to our displays or lawn ornaments. I'm fine with all of that.

In fact, I had already planned on buying a few new items to add to my Christmas décor later this year. And I was even looking forward to celebrating the birth of our Lord and Savior in the month of December—when it was cold outside, like it should be when drinking hot apple cider or cocoa by a roaring fire.

I wasn't even going to complain about the malls bringing out their decorations before Halloween later this year.

But in June?

That's too much. Even though the actual celebration will be on July twenty-fifth, it feels like everyone is going nuts six weeks early.

How is it that I'm the only one who thinks this way? I don't know a single person who hasn't already put up their lights and lawn ornaments this year. The day after Gina did her post, the entire world began dragging out their Christmas displays.

And the sales began...

A shiver ran down my spine as I looked around the outdoor mall. Not a single store was bare. They all had signs advertising their sales and were decorated to the hilt for Christmas. Did I leave planet Earth and end up in Dr. Seuss's *How the Grinch Stole Christmas*? The one with the live actors and the cutest little girl playing Cindy-Lou Who? I keep seeing the opening scene in my head, where the dad who works for the local post office is dragging his little girl around to Christmas shop.

All around me, mothers and fathers dragged their kids along with bags and boxes of gifts and décor weighing everyone down. In that one moment, I could understand where the Grinch was coming from.

This wasn't what the meaning of Christmas was all about. This was commercialization, plain and simple. Sure, I loved to give and get gifts just like everyone else at Christmas. But I had this sign I put up every year to remind me that Christmas wasn't about the presents—it was about His presence. There really was a difference.

Okay, okay, don't hate me. I loved Santa. My aunt even told me years ago that if I didn't believe in Santa, I wouldn't get presents. So, I believed. But I also remembered the true meaning. It was a time to celebrate the birth of my Lord and Savior Jesus Christ.

I could still have fun with all of the festive decorations, parties, and quirky sweaters. There was nothing wrong with having fun, as long as we didn't forget. These people who were charging their credit cards to the max, pushing in lines, and being rude? They either didn't know the true reason for the season, or they'd forgotten.

"Oomph." I breathed out as some strange lady with red-and-white stripes in what appeared to be originally be blond hair bumped past me.

She glared at me. "Watch it, lady. Some of us are here to shop."

So, maybe I was standing in the middle of the shopping mall gawking at the craziness, but I wasn't the one who bumped into her. I was standing still and she bumped into me. She should have apologized or moved away from me.

A deep sigh escaped as I realized that today wasn't going to be a good day. The sun was shining, but if birds were chirping, I couldn't hear them. And if they were, they were probably complaining about the walking candy cane who lacked manners.

This all cemented my thoughts from last night... *I'm not going to celebrate Christmas in July.*

Instead, I turned to the store I needed—the Ladies' Dress Boutique—and prayed I'd survive getting a new sundress for the upcoming pool party at my parents' house next weekend.

I should have known that God had turned his back on my petitions to go back in time and erase Gina's tweet. In fact, I had asked God to take her account away from her, but he'd ignored my plea. Just as well. My request wasn't exactly altruistic; it was selfish, and I knew it. But I asked anyway.

Now, if I could survive the Black Friday of '18, I could survive this one. That year there were three fights in our Wal-Mart, all while I was there. I'd made it out safely, to my mother's disbelief. Usually if there's trouble, I'm right in the middle of it.

My mom has always said, "Millie, trouble follows you like flies on stink."

She's not wrong.

I started keeping journals in high school of all of my, um...shall we say, mishaps. After I filled the fifth one, I quit keeping a journal. Then, when I successfully graduated high school without tripping once during graduation, I decided my journals needed to be gone. My best friend and I went to the beach and had a nice, toasty bonfire in the middle of June.

It was hot.

All five of my journals burned on the altar of, "Let's forget high school and move on to college." Jeanie agreed with me. It was time to put that trouble in the past and move on.

Sadly, my luck followed me.

And it seemed it wasn't going away any time soon.

Chapter 2

Millie

You know those movies where the heroine is totally kick-butt and can see an accident coming from a mile away and she avoids it with grace and aplomb? Yeah, that's not me.

Not even close.

I should have seen this day coming, but I didn't.

Instead, I walked straight into the eye of the storm and didn't even realize the worst was yet to come.

Normally, this particular boutique dress shop had two clerks and never more than four or five patrons at a time. Their dresses were on the pricier side. Not that I was rich, but the quality was worth the price. I had several outfits from this store that looked as though I'd bought them last week, when in reality I'd bought them almost seven years ago.

This was *not* your local five and dime.

Although, I wasn't afraid to admit that I shopped those stores, too. But for my mother's pool party, I needed a quality dress that would stand up to whatever my bad luck could throw at me. No matter how hard I tried, I always, and I mean *always*, spilled something on the front of my clothes. Or sat on someone's discarded paper plate.

So when I found myself standing in front of the door to the boutique, shock spread through my system like ice-cold water in my veins. I hesitated opening the door until someone shoved their way out and pushed me to the side. I barely managed to stay upright and not fall into the overwatered planter next to the front door.

After I got out the way of the rude patron, I saw what could only be described as hell inside. I took a deep breath and gave myself a little pep talk. "Time to gird your loins and be a big girl. You need this new dress, and this store is the best. You can do this. So what if women are acting more like toddlers throwing a hissy fit than grown women?"

I straightened my shoulders and walked inside with confidence. Only to turn around when one lady pushed me into a table with one lemon chiffon blouse left...size extra small, of course.

Did I mention being a...uh...full-figured lady? I wouldn't go so far as to call myself fat, but if I were to model, I'd be called a plus-sized model. Even though I wore a size twelve and was five feet, nine inches tall. The fashion industry was cruel.

But I happened to like the way I looked in flowing dresses. Especially ones with pretty prints on them. A month ago, they had a dress in the window that was a pale pink with large daisies on it and very elegant cap sleeves. The skirt looked as though it would go to about the middle of my calves. It would most likely cover the areas of my thighs I wasn't proud of and show off my arms. I'd spent a lot of time over the past year working on my arms, and they looked good, if I said so myself.

My plan was to find the dress and buy it without even trying it on. Did I mention today was basically the June version of November's Black Friday? Massive sales everywhere, including this boutique, which was why I could afford to buy the dress.

Turned out, I wasn't the only one who felt that way.

I started to leave the store and noticed the dress I wanted out of the corner of my eye. It was on a rack in the corner. Several women had their backs to the rack while they argued over who was going to get the last red dress they were all ogling.

Instead of leaving, I tried to make my way to the dress. My dress. Which was easier said than done. A running back would have had a difficult time getting around all of the obstacles these women threw my way. It felt as though a horde of linemen were trying to tackle me as I made my way down the playing field, attempting to score a touchdown.

Actually, playing in any major-league sport would have been easier than shopping in that store.

I dodged to the left, then spun around and to the right to escape a flying arm reaching for some scarf on a table I just happened to pass by. Why couldn't these women show the tiniest bit of respect?

After dodging multiple elbows and purses thrown my way, along with a few yelling women, I made it to the corner and grabbed the last dress in my size. It was the exact one I'd seen in the window. For the first time since I'd arrived at the mall, I smiled and exhaled. I'd done it. I found the dress and didn't die in the process.

If only I'd run the second I touched that hanger.

Before my smile even had time to make it all the way to my eyes, someone shoved me against the wall.

"Outta my way! Can't you see I've got an armful of dresses to buy?" The rude women scoffed and ran away.

What I wanted to say was, "Yeah, sure, I have eyes in the back of my head and saw you coming a mile away. Sorry I didn't move out of your way, seeing as how you're an elephant and I'm a lonely meerkat, I totally could have and should have moved."

Instead, what came out was a series of not-so-nice words that my mother would have washed my mouth out for uttering. Although, I doubted anyone could hear the muffled words considering my mouth was pushed up against the wall.

Ewww...gross. I never considered what the wall of a dress shop might taste like. Never again would I have to wonder. Actually, I hoped I'd never remember this day. If I had some Calgon, I'd be saying, "Calgon, take me away," the entire trip home. Maybe I had a bath bomb left over from last year? That might smooth out the kinks in my muscles after this trip.

As I tore myself off the wall, another woman bumped me. But at least she apologized. Never mind that she didn't bother looking my way, but at least she yelled out, "Sorry." I was amazed at how she never even lost her stride.

Instead of getting in the line snaking across the store and down around three times, I threw my hands in the air and the dress escaped my clutches. It was a total accident, I swear. I never meant to start anything, or even to have women look my way.

The moment the dress went in the air, you'd think a horde of elephants was rampaging through the store. Yells of all sorts went out, even a few that deserved to be censored. And the women pounced on my dress.

I didn't care. I was going to go home, see if the dress was available online, and would be happy to pay for overnight shipping, if that was what it took to get it on time. In fact, until the world calmed down, I wasn't setting foot in the mall again.

Now, the only problem left...how to escape with my life.

Or at least, my hair not getting pulled out.

Chapter 3

Corbin

Today was a typical Southern California beautiful day. The sun was shining, it wasn't even in the eighties yet, but it would get there after lunch. A light breeze wafted from the fronds of the tall palm trees lining the streets in most Southern California neighborhoods. It was the perfect time to take my Boston Terrier Bella out for a walk, and to head to the mall for just the right Christmas Hawaiian-print shirt. I had a party to attend next weekend.

Since the world had decided to celebrate Christmas in July, I'd decided to go full throttle. Instead of ugly sweater parties, it was Hawaiian-print Christmas shirts at pool parties. This was going to be a blast. I only had the one Santa Hawaiian shirt, which I was wearing, and decided I should see how many more I could pick up. One could never have too many Hawaiian-print shirts when you lived near the beach.

Bella and I lived and worked in a smart, three-story artist's work loft in Corona, California. That's Corona, *no* Del Mar. And we certainly aren't the beer capital, thank you very much. And don't even mention that virus; we are so totally *not* the city of the virus. For those who don't know, Corona means "crown" in Spanish. And with the Spanish and Mexican influences in Southern California, it made complete sense to our founding fathers.

Growing up here, I loved the idea that I lived in a city named "Crown." Now, not so much. At least Corona Del Mar had the beach. We had the smog and traffic rotten enough to scare away even the heartiest of humans. When I worked in Orange County, I lived out there. But the first chance I got to start my own consulting business had me moving back to the city I loved. Now, I lived and worked in Corona. Most of my family was still here as well.

Now, my commute was a one-minute walk downstairs to my studio. Granted, this complex was first developed with artists in mind, but lately we'd seen quite a few self-employed, business-minded people moving in. The bottom floor was exclusively a work area. I had my office and a reception area designed to welcome in clients when they wanted to meet me at my office. Normally I'd meet at their office, or on Zoom. However, by having this space solely dedicated to work, I got to write off part of the costs for my loft. And I got to walk to most places I needed, including the quaint farmers' market in the high-end shopping mall and the Trader Joe's market.

As Bella and I walked to the local outdoor mall, we passed other residents out and about with their dogs, or just out enjoying the nice weather. One good thing about the change in work lately was that more and more people were working from home, like I was. And we could take the occasional long lunch or short break to go for a walk.

I nodded to those I didn't know and stopped to shoot the breeze with those I did. Living here in this little oasis that had just about anything I needed made it more like a hamlet. In Southern California, most people didn't talk to strangers. But in Corona, we did. I'd missed my city when I was gone.

Whoever came up with Christmas in July was a genius. There was no other word to describe this outstanding idea. Last December when the world was all shut up, and just about everyone missed out on Christmas. We weren't allowed to meet up with family, even if we weren't sick. I'll admit, I did go to my parents' house on December twenty-fifth for a subdued Christmas dinner. We had a few gifts for each other, but it was just the three of us.

And it didn't feel like Christmas. I know, the day is supposed to be about celebrating the birth of our Lord and Savior, but it was hard to be joyous when everyone else around us was so miserable. Thankfully, the three of us never got that virus. But we knew too many who did get it, and some who went home to be with the Lord.

Normally, our Christmas Day included at least twenty people. My parents had a nice-sized home, and they held a Christmas open house. In a non-virus year, all of our friends and neighbors were invited to come over. Those who didn't have family in the area would come over. It was never quiet or lonely on Christmas Day at my house growing up.

Until this last year...

However, we weren't the only ones who felt the sadness and loneliness of being quarantined. But now, with everyone out and about and healthy again, life felt more...alive. I had more energy than I'd had in a long time. Not to mention how much humanity was embracing Christmas. It wasn't "Happy Holidays" now—it was actually "Merry Christmas." Some were adding "in July" to the end of their greeting, but it didn't matter. All that mattered was everyone, and I mean *everyone*, wanted to celebrate the most wonderful time of the year.

Last night on the news, they had a segment in Australia with the families and children loving how chilly it was Down Under. They finally got to celebrate Christmas like we did. And we'd finally get to understand what it was like to hang out in swim trunks on the beach with a Santa wearing an old-time, red-and-white striped swimming suit from what must have been the Regency era. I could imagine Santa on an English beach in the summer wearing this getup and not being out of place.

The kids were going wild for Santa in his swimsuit. And Mrs. Claus has a matching one with a white lacey cap, similar to what the older ladies in that *Pride and Prejudice* movie wore. Yes, I once sat down for the entire five-hour BBC presentation of *Pride and Prejudice* from Jane Austen. I dated a woman who was totally into the Regency era. I'd seen at least three versions of that movie, but even I knew that the BBC one was the best. However...let's keep this between us. If any of my guy friends knew I had a preference for a *Pride and Prejudice* movie, I'd lose all masculine credibility.

Anyway, it was a beautiful day and I was out shopping. I'd heard there was going to be a huge sale today. Maybe the stores had stocked up on Santa-print shirts? It would be fun to spend the next few weeks sporting Santa on a surfboard, or Santa building a sand castle-style snowman. I heard that some of the beaches were even going to have snowman contests. Of course, the snowmen were to be made out of sand, so maybe they were calling them sandmen?

I shivered when I thought about it too hard. I just couldn't see the fun in making sandmen. It would constantly remind me of the song, which would then remind me of the poem. Nope, they would be snowmen. Just made from sand instead of snow.

Without even realizing it, I began whistling a tune. I almost stopped when I realized it was a Christmas one. Then I started to sing "Frosty the Snowman." It did feel a bit odd to be singing about snow at the beginning of summer. But who cared? Several people smiled and waved at me as I continued to sing my merry way to the mall.

As my steps lightened, I figured I might even watch one of those sentimental Hallmark Christmas movies. I'd probably stick to the military ones, as those could be explained away as military movies and not romances. No one would ever suspect I was being sappy. Everything about the season brightened my outlook on life. I wasn't normally the type to go all out for Christmas. Sure, I loved it—the food, the gifts, and the special services at church helped to make the season brighter. But this year, there was something more.

A sense of hope, peace, and yes, joy permeated the air. I couldn't remember when I'd seen so many happy faces before. Everyone smiled at me and Bella as they passed, even if they didn't say anything. And yes, my dog was wearing a cute Santa hat designed for small dogs, but that was the extent of her doggy costumes these days.

I almost scowled when I remembered that Halloween right before the pandemic hit. Then I laughed. It was actually funny to watch, but poor Bella. I was a horrible human to her. No dog should have to attempt wearing doggy skates. I don't even know why companies make and sell them.

Bella must have known what I was laughing about, as she turned her little Boston Terrier version of a scowl on me and barked.

"I know, I know. I'm sorry. No skates for you." I waggled my index finger at my little black-and-white dog, who nodded and looked forward again.

Poor baby. She'd never shied away from anything I wanted to do. She loved catching Frisbees, balls, and was pretty good at fetch. But when her little legs spread out in all directions, I hurt for the girl.

All I could think of was the time when Bernie Hanson was six years old and he tried to put those funky skates on over his tennis shoes. His feet went out from under him and he ended up doing the splits. No six-year-old boy should ever be forced into the splits. I don't think he left his house for days.

I can still hear the piercing sound of his cry for help.

Okay, on to better thoughts. Christmas in July. Oh, peppermint candy. Maybe I'd see if the candy store in the mall had any peppermints. That sounded yummy. My stomach rumbled its approval and I picked up the pace. A cup of joe and a peppermint candy would hit the spot nicely when we made it to the shopping center.

"Bella, would you like to try a shirt? Maybe a matching Hawaiian-print shirt for dogs?" I wondered if they even made such a thing, and decided I'd give the pet store a try if the clothing store I was headed to didn't have matching dog apparel. That might be an idea; an online store for pet lovers would do extremely well. Maybe if my marketing business failed, I could open one up.

Now, my dog could possibly be described as a bit of a prima donna. She turned her head toward me and barked, then turned back around and pranced along next to me as though she was the Queen of Sheba incarnate.

Huh, maybe I should cut back on the amount of love and attention I doled out to my dog? Could her attitude be a result of spoiling her? I shook my head. "Nah, that's not possible, is it?" We stopped and I bent down to pet my little girl. "Who's a pretty girl?" I nodded and scratched behind her ear. "That's right, you're my pretty girl."

Bella licked my hand and then pulled on my leash. She loved the shopping mall. It was one of those outdoor types, the kind where dogs were welcomed. They even had a small grassy area for dogs to do their business. All over the complex were little boxes that were always full of doggy bags, for those who forgot to bring their own. There was also a small trashcan next to the dispensers.

I always made sure I had at least four bags in the little baggie carrier in Bella's leash before I left the house. We should never be caught out without a means to dispose of Bella's trash. But it was generous of the center to provide bags for those who didn't think far enough ahead.

Today was going to be one of those busy days. It was a good thing I worked for myself and didn't have any meetings the rest of the day. As we walked into the mall, the place was packed. Cars were everywhere. Horns were honking, and people were in long lines, some of which snaked out of the stores.

Since I wanted to hit up a couple of stores, I decided to check and see which one had the shortest line. It wasn't that I minded being in a crowd, but the Christmas ambiance could be a little much for Bella. Since she was so small, only fifteen pounds, people didn't always see her. I had to watch out for feet that might not move. Then, when people did notice Bella, they always stooped down to pet her.

This year, it was going to be fun.

I loved watching the Christmas Crazy ladies. They were a hoot. If ever you wanted free entertainment, head out to the mall and take a seat. Be sure to get a large soda and popcorn. People-watching during the biggest sales of the year always made me laugh. It was funny how they fought over the silliest things.

Most of the products were on sale online nowadays, so there really wasn't a need to go all wacko on everyone. Usually I looked at the Black

Friday ads and then placed my orders online. Sometimes I'd go into the stores, if they had something in-store only, but that was rare nowadays.

Today, well...most stores probably hadn't had time to set up the online sales. Or they didn't have enough inventory to do it all online. Which was why I'd come here instead of ordering online; I knew the selection would be better in person. If I didn't find what I wanted, then I'd try the online beach apparel stores and pay for overnight shipping.

A laugh burst forth when I saw two women in line for the candy store arguing about who'd gotten there first. One lady looked as though she was about to blow her top. Her face was red, and I swear she had steam coming out of her head. This was just the sort of entertainment that warranted a large soda and popcorn. I was definitely going to have to make time in my schedule for Christmas Crazy-watching.

When I took two steps to the right, I realized it was just steam from the food cart behind the fighting duo. Well, that deflated my enjoyment, but only a little.

"Bella, are you up for this?" I grinned at my little dog. Her tongue was lolling, and I realized she had her sights, and probably her nose, set on the hot-dog cart sending steaming scents of delicious processed meat over those ladies' heads. "Alright, you be good and I'll get you a hot dog after I get my shirts."

The dog looked up at me and tilted her head, as though she understood what I'd said and was considering her options. Then she barked and looked forward again, waiting for me to tell her where to go.

"That's a good girl." I guided us to the Aloha Hawaii store in the middle of the mall. The entertainment along the way was almost enough to get me to stop and sit for a while. I did still have some work that needed to get done for a client of mine in Taiwan, so I had some time, but not much. However, we moved on and I went into the Aloha Hawaii store.

After browsing the racks, I did indeed find two new Santa surf Hawaiian-print shirts and one seascape snowman shirt. I wasn't sure if these were new designs or something the manufacturers had in stock for those Down Under, but I was happy. I might even go so far as to say I was Christmas Happy.

Not to be confused with Christmas Crazy.

While Bella and I stood in a long line wrapping around the store, we chatted with the couple standing in front of us. Then two elderly women fanning themselves got in line behind me with a variety of summer Christmas shirts. This store was a gold mine for Christmas in July.

"Martha, I've never," one octogenarian with a very tall gray head of hair stated as she continued fanning her red face.

I looked at the lady who appeared about ready to pass out and smiled. She ignored me, or maybe she couldn't see me over the gray poof of her friend's tall hair. The two elderly women looked to be from a movie set on the beach in the fifties. Both had tall bouffant-style hair; one was gray while the other was pink. I couldn't be sure if she had it dyed pink, or if a cotton-candy machine had exploded on her head. Either way, it looked a lot like spun sugar sitting high atop her head.

The lady with the cotton-candy hair replied, "Betty, we should have known today wasn't going to be the right day to shop."

"But fighting over dresses in a high-end shop?" Betty tsked and shook her head. "In our day, one would never have behaved so horribly."

Pink-haired Martha pursed her lips and finally noticed me. "Young man, what has gotten into your generation?"

While I did want to speak with them, I certainly didn't want to be accused of whatever they were talking about. "Excuse me, ma'am, I'm not sure what you're asking me."

Martha looked at her gray-haired friend and then motioned around her. "This...this...I don't even know what to call it. But this nonsense over dresses. Grown women were fighting over dresses in the store two doors down." She harumphed.

I didn't think I'd ever met anyone who had harumphed. Sure, I'd seen it on TV, but never in person. *Huh*. It wasn't as impactful as I would have imagined. "I think you mean the Christmas Crazy?"

Both ladies nodded, and their hair moved like a Jell-O mold my old Aunt Gertrude used to bring to our Christmas dinners before she passed on. No one ever ate it, but she thought everyone loved it.

I think the dogs ate it. That must have been why our old German Shepherd used to get indigestion every holiday meal. For the Fourth of July, Gertrude would bring a patriotic one. I wasn't sure how she got the red, white, and blue to separate perfectly as it did, but it was pretty to look at when the sun shone on it just right as it wiggled in the breeze. Our dog always ate it, too. She must have known it would make her sick, but she didn't care. Maybe Aunt Gertrude did know the truth and she put a doggy treat in the middle? A little *something* to ensure that someone ate her Jell-O mold? That might be what always got Lolly, our German Shepherd, to go Jell-O mold crazy.

I missed Aunt Gertrude. She would have loved this Christmas in July. Maybe I could get my mom to make a Jell-O mold in her memory this year.

The two women brought me back to the present, and I smiled. They were bickering over who'd seen the worst fight.

"I'm telling you, that woman had a bloody nose. There's no way another woman hadn't knocked her around just to get a dress that was only thirty percent off." Martha moved the clothes in her arms around.

"Here, let me hold those for you." I reached out with my hand that held Bella's leash for the three shirts the elderly woman was having difficulty carrying.

Martha put them in my hand. Then she pinched my cheek like I was a little six-year-old who'd brought her a butterscotch candy. Yes, my grandmother used to do that. And yes, I still hated the memory. Not of my grandmother, but of the pinched cheeks. It wasn't something boys of any age liked. And certainly not something men approved of.

As we waited our turn in line, we chatted about how crazy everyone was.

"I swear, most people stayed cooped up for so long, they no longer know how to act in public." Betty pursed her lips and looked out the window as a man bumped into a woman, who didn't take too kindly to being knocked to the side. She really should have been looking where she was going. And he should have as well.

From my somewhat insulated vantage point inside the store, the outside looked more like oversized ants crawling all over the concrete walk searching in earnest for food—or in this case, great deals before they all expired. I had to turn away when Bella whimpered.

I followed her gaze. She had located another shirt that would be perfect for the next month, at least. "Martha, Betty, would you mind holding my spot while I check out that shirt?" I pointed to the rack holding what looked to be another fun and silly Christmas in July shirt.

"Of course, dear. I can take your dog's leash if you like." Martha held out her hand for Bella's leash.

"Thanks." I stooped down and scratched behind Bella's ear. "Now you behave for these nice ladies and when we get outside, I won't forget about that hot dog I promised you earlier."

Bella let out a light chuff, signaling her agreement, then licked my face. One thing I've learned with dogs is they all know the word "hot dog." Every one of the dogs I've had throughout my life enjoyed those tasty treats. Even more than a doggy patty at In-N-Out. Bella would never turn her nose up at anything so tasty, but she did seem to prefer the hot dogs. I couldn't blame her; the processed meat was truly tasty.

When I made it to the rack, I couldn't keep my chuckle in. On the front of the green Christmas shirt was an ironed-on image of a Santa Claus on the beach in one of those old-timey, red-and-white swimsuits. He was holding a glass bottle of Coca-Cola and had a giant smile on his face. The caption under the image was, *It's an Aussie thing*. I had to have it. Thankfully, they had my size.

I grinned at the two women who had taken care of Bella, and when I got back in line I realized we were almost to the register. It didn't take too much longer to pay for my items and walk out of the store feeling like I was ready for whatever was heading my way.

I really shouldn't have tempted fate like that.

I should have known the moment I thought I had everything heading in the right direction, something would go wrong. Bella and I went to the hot-dog booth and we each got a dog with no issues. Of course, I don't give Bella the bun—she only got the meat. And without any toppings. While I busied myself fixing my dog with mustard and relish, she gobbled up her treat and was sitting there looking at me with those irresistible eyes, begging for my own hot dog.

It was a good thing I knew how bad bread and condiments were for her, or she would have ended up with mine as well.

Not a few minutes later I thought, *Hmm, maybe I should have given it to her after all.*

"What? Millie?" I looked on in horror as a woman who very much resembled my childhood best friend, was shoved through the door and landed on her face in the mud. Actually, it was more like a middle-school boy doing a belly flop into a tiny backyard pool full of mud.

When she landed, the muddy water that should have never been sitting idly in that planter, splashed up and out like the wave of a belly flop. I couldn't believe there was that much mud and water in the planter. Didn't those things only have a few inches of ground covering? Or did they not put any cement under the tiny plants dotting the dirt?

I felt the lightness in my hand and realized I had dropped my hot dog at my feet. But I couldn't care about the food as one of my oldest friends lay there not two feet from me drenched in the brown goo that covered the planter outside the dress shop.

Since I only got three bites before the incident, Bella might have been better off with my hot dog. Instead it was sitting at my feet, and mustard and relish covered the front of my Santa Hawaiian-print shirt. Did mustard stains come out in the wash?

Great, now there was also mud all down the front of me.

Even Bella ignored the hot dog in favor of staring at the woman in the mud.

But no, it couldn't be Millie. Even she wouldn't have fallen face first into an overflowing planter full of mud and discarded trash. Or could she?

And for Pete's sake, hadn't everyone learned by now to ensure sprinkler heads worked properly? We were still facing a multi-year drought, after all. The planter box beneath the front window of the store was overflowing with water and mud. Not to mention the poor woman lying there, spluttering.

Chapter 4

Millie

My last coherent thought was how to escape with my hair follicles intact. Perhaps I should have wondered how to escape with my life? I swear, I don't even know how it all happened. One second I was standing by the exit trying to extricate myself from a group of crazy women fighting over something, then I was pushed outside and had my face smashed into the rectangle muddy planter in front of the window.

It felt like a wrestling move I'd seen on TV. One woman pushed another down onto the mat, pushing her face further and further into the mat. Only in this case, it was the muddy planter, and it felt as though someone shoved my face deeper and deeper into the grossness of the wet dirt. Didn't matter that there wasn't a woman sitting on top of me, it only felt like it.

Could life get any worse?

Yes, yes it could.

And it did. But I didn't know it at first.

As I spluttered mud and some sort of plant debris and God only knew what else out of my mouth, a set of strong arms reached under my pits and pulled me up. If I had known whose strong arms those were, I would have preferred to lie there drowning in a brown mush of dirty mud.

"Here, let me help you." A voice I recognized sent tendrils of anxiety throughout my entire being.

This man was someone I had artfully avoided for years. Not only had he been witness to some of my most embarrassing situations in high school, but now he was also witness to my latest. The Christmas Crazy ladies had done it—I was now thoroughly and completely done with Christmas this year. Maybe even forever.

The idea of going to my mother's pool party next weekend was completely out of the question.

The man took a shirt out of his bag and handed it to me. "Sorry, I don't have a handkerchief or napkins to help you, but the shirt is brand new and should help you to wipe that...uh...gunk off your face." I could hear a sense of dread enter his voice. He must have recognized me. "I'm sorry, where are my manners? I'm Corbin Deeks. And this is my dog, Bella."

So he hadn't recognized me, yet. Maybe I could get away before he saw my face. I took the shirt, held it up in front of me, and wiped away the goop from my eyes so I could at least see where I was going. "Thanks, I'll get your shirt back to you."

Not wanting him to see me, or even realize who I was, I turned and started to head out to my car. At this point, all I wanted was to get inside to the safety of my own house and hibernate all through summer. Yeah, yeah, I know. Winter is the hibernation season. Summer is when everyone is out and about. But I think the real reason for hibernation is that the bears want to avoid Christmas Crazy. And now, I want to avoid Christmas Crazy in July.

Corbin's voice was hesitant as he called my name. "Millie? Is it really you?"

I stopped with my back to him and hung my head. At my feet, Bella was sniffing my shoes. Then she sat up, and with her tongue lolling to the side, she grinned. I know, dogs don't grin. But Bella did. While I had done my best to steer clear of Corbin, I had seen Bella on many occasions when Corbin's parents were dog-sitting for him when he had to go out of town on business.

I loved Bella. She was one of the sweetest dogs I'd ever met. Resigning myself to the inevitable, I leaned down and almost put a muddy hand on Bella's head. "Hey girl. Sorry I can't pet you right now. I don't think you'd appreciate the mud." Then I stood up and turned around to face the music. "Long time, no see."

"Millie? Is that really you?" Corbin scratched his head and stared at me, blinking.

"Ah, yes, it is." It wasn't like I could lie and say I was someone else. Knowing Corbin the way I did, he'd follow me to my car and then he'd know for sure it was me. As much as I wanted to hide my identity, I couldn't. If I could find a way to kick myself in the backside for opening my mouth, I would.

Normally I was much better at hiding from him. Maybe all the mud in my mouth translated to mud in the brains? I didn't know what had happened with the planter, but I could have disguised my voice and he wouldn't have known who I was.

"Are you alright?" Corbin moved closer to me and put out a hand, but it recoiled when he realized how muddy I was.

"I'm fine. I just need a good long soak in the tub." Seriously, Calgon, where are you when I need you? I'd probably need two showers and *then* a long soak in the tub to get all this grime off my body. "Hmph." A cough emerged when I tried a dramatic harumph like I'd seen in those silly movies. My clothes? They were heading for the trash heap.

"What happened? Did you fall prey to the Christmas Crazy?" He held up a hand. "Wait, please tell me you aren't one of those crazy shoppers? Was it you who busted a woman's nose over a dress?"

If I could have laughed without coughing up a mouth full of mud, I might have. I saw the brawl he'd just described. Thankfully, I wasn't close enough to those crazy ladies to be a part of it. One woman ended up with a bloody nose while the other looked like she was going to have a nice shiner to show for her shopping excursion. "No, I wasn't involved." *Thankfully*.

At least one disaster today wasn't my fault. Although, this planter incident wasn't my fault, not really. I was totally innocent, just in the wrong place at the wrong time. The story of my life whenever Corbin Deeks was near.

After the first bit of trouble, I should have known he was somewhere close by. I never got into scrapes like this unless he was around to witness it. This was high school all over again.

Now that he knew who I was, I might as well wipe as much goop off my face as best I could. Using the shirt he'd given me, I wiped a huge glob of mud off of me and onto the ground. "Sorry, I'll clean it and give it to your mother next time I'm in the neighborhood." Which wouldn't be for at least another forty-five days. Since I had already decided to avoid Christmas in July, I'd make sure I didn't go anywhere at all until August.

Since it was just a t-shirt, I doubted he'd need it any time soon.

"I'll be at your parents' pool party next weekend," Corbin said. "I could get it back from you then."

I groaned. Of course he was invited, and would attend. Our parents were old friends and neighbors. His family was always invited to every event my parents held, and vice versa.

"Miss, you're gonna have to come with me," another voice, one I didn't recognize, said from behind me.

Confused, I turned around and looked at the mall's rent-a-cop. Probably hired for the Christmas shopping season. "Huh? Why?" I was fine enough to make it home on my own. I could see. Well, see enough to walk out to my car where I had some wet wipes and could clean my face off well enough to get safely home from there.

Well, as long as Corbin Deeks wasn't anywhere near me I could drive safely. I swear, that boy—I mean man, or was it man-child? Anyway, he always brought out the worst of luck for me.

"You walked out of the store without paying for that purse." He pointed to my hand. "And now it's destroyed."

I looked down at my right hand and all I saw was the crumpled-up shirt that Corbin had handed me, now caked in mud. I'd seen him take it out of his own shopping bag. But wait, didn't the rent-a-cop say purse? Then it dawned on me, and I looked at my left wrist. Strapped around it was what had once been a pretty little sunflower wristlet. It would have gone nicely with the dress I'd come here to buy. Now? It was a mess. Not even a hot mess, just a mess of crumpled yellow cornhusks sticking every which way with mud caked all over it. Nothing was going to clean this up.

"But...but..." I spluttered. "I didn't walk out of the store. I was pushed out."

"Right, and it wasn't you that started the stampede over the flowery dress?" The young guy put his hands on his utility belt that held a menacing flashlight and radio. He actually stood like he thought he was a real cop in one of those TV shows. Like he had a gun on his belt instead of a radio, or a baton instead of a flashlight. Who did he think he was, T.J. Hooker? Wait, that's not a fair comparison. William Shatner was much better looking as a beat cop. No, this punk was more like Chief Wiggum from *The Simpsons*. Was that a pink donut crumb on his name tag?

I squinted when the sun hit my eyes and turned so it wasn't directly burning my corneas. "It wasn't me. Look"—I put a mud-covered hand on my hip—"I was trying to leave the store thanks to the Christmas crazies. I had planned on going home and just buying what I needed online."

"Look, lady, I don't have time to argue with you. Let's go. I'm taking you in." The wannabe cop put his hand out to grab my arm.

Corbin stood between us. "Hold up. I saw her getting pushed out the door." He motioned to his shirt. "And I have some of my own damage, thanks to the crazy ladies. Not"—he pointed to me—"her."

"Sorry, sir, but she left the store without paying for the purse. I've already got a call into the police. They're sending someone over. If you want to lodge a complaint against the lady for ruining your sweet shirt, you can join us at the mall office." Barney Fife reached for my arm, but I moved it out of his way and began walking just to ensure he didn't touch me.

"I'll pay for the purse that was destroyed. There's no need to involve the police. If there's a video somewhere, I'm sure you'll see that it was all part of the craziness of this sale." Corbin pointed to a camera near the door.

We all looked, and I was amazed he had noticed it. I never had paid enough attention to the building to see the camera. And I was shocked he was trying to help me. The shock and confusion must have been what caused my mouth to open and close like a fish out of water instead of standing up for myself. I could have easily paid for the purse, even at full price. I would have, too, if given the chance.

In fact, I looked at the boy's name tag. The guy couldn't have been out of his teens yet. If he was over twenty, I was a size two. "Look, Mark? I can pay for this purse. I had no intention of leaving the store without paying for it. In fact, I was just checking it out so I could go and buy it online when I got home. That line—" I pointed back through the door and noticed that several of the women who had been fighting were now gawking at me.

Great, now I was going to be known as the mud-covered shoplifter.

I shook my head and looked back at the stupid mall security guard. "I wasn't about to stand in that long line while women literally threw punches at each other. Actually, why are you bugging me for a fifty-dollar bag when there are women in there bleeding? You should go back and stop those fights, and I'll drop off the money at the register."

"No can do." The mall cop rocked back and forth on his heels and grinned at me as though I was the big catch of the day. For him, I probably was.

Ten minutes later, all three of us—correction, all four of us—were in the tiny mall security office waiting for the police to arrive. I counted Bella. Of everyone present, she was the only one who liked me. So she counted.

"Can't I at least wash my face?"

I had asked if he would let me go home and shower before dealing with all of this. I even offered to leave my driver's license with him.

The boy pursed his lips and looked me up and down. "Yeah, there's a sink back there. Go ahead and clean up as best you can." He pointed to a door that must have led to the break room.

As I walked away, I mentally went through who all I knew that might be up for a hit job. This kid needed to go. But before I could truly think about it, I overheard Corbin trying to get me out of this again. What was with him? Why did he want to help me so badly?

"Ah!" I screamed when I looked in the mirror. If I hadn't known better, I would have sworn the creature from the black lagoon was looking back at me. I couldn't even tell my own brown locks from the muddy blobs hanging around my head.

"What's wrong?" Corbin said when he barreled into the little break room.

"Nothing. I just, ah, looked in the mirror." I narrowed my eyes at my nemesis. "Why didn't you warn me I looked so scary?"

Corbin's face fell, and he and Bella both tried to scurry out of the room before I could get to them.

When the door closed, I turned back around and looked at the counter to see what I had to work with.

There was definitely no need for me to lift my arms and smell. I could already tell it was going to be an awful stench. My nose twitched just thinking about it. There was also no need for me to lower my chin to my chest and take a whiff. I just knew without a shadow of a doubt it would also be outlandish. The sort of thing that would get me booted from any shop or restaurant, let alone a society maiden's front doorstep.

I was just grateful for the stylish capris I'd worn today.

"Oh, figgy pudding." I modulated my voice this time so no would hear me. "What would have happened if I'd worn my dress? Nope, not going there."

"Ow." A twinge of pain hit my hip, then my arm. I looked down, but with all the mud on me I couldn't tell what had caused the pain.

With my luck, a brown recluse spider had probably bitten me. We had those here in Corona, right?

It couldn't be happening again. Just like in high school, I made a total and complete fool of myself in front of the hottest guy I'd ever known. A guy my heart still pounded for. When I saw him standing there above me, my stupid organ kicked up it's beat as though it was a hoedown, and we were doing some sort of country line dance.

How much time did I have before the police arrived?

Chapter 5

14 years earlier

Millie

Tonight was the night Corbin Deeks would *finally* see me as a woman. If I had to sit through one more society event where everyone commented on how they thought we were brother and sister, I was going to punch something—or someone. Sure, Corbin and I had grown up together. Our parents were best friends and neighbors our entire lives. But come on, we *weren't* related. Not even a teeny tiny bit.

However, he was the hot football player at our high school. While I wasn't exactly a wallflower, most likely thanks to my friendship with Corbin I also wasn't the head cheerleader, or a cheerleader at all. In fact, that set completely ignored me when Corbin was around. All of the girls at school wanted Corbin.

And why not? He was athletic, popular, smart, and nice to everyone. Including the wallflowers. At the last school dance, he actually went up to Tracy Anderson and asked her to dance! No one ever asked Tracy to dance. In fact, most people didn't even know who she was.

The only reason I did was because we were lab partners in biology last year.

I was an inbetweener. Not truly popular, but also not a nobody. I was on the fringes of popularity. Dating Corbin would make my reputation. But that wasn't why I wanted him to see me for who I was now. No, it was something else.

"Oh, Millie. You're totally going to get Corbin's attention tonight." Jeanie jumped up and down in her two-inch gold heels and her black slinky dress that showed off her tan arms and perfect calves. She was a dancer, and on the fringes like me.

Jeanie and I were best friends. However, she had a boyfriend, and I didn't. She'd probably end up marrying the guy, Browning. He was a football player, but second string and rarely played. He too was on the fringes, but always invited everywhere since he was a football player.

"Do you really think so?" I looked into the mirror at myself. Jeanie had done a fantastic job fixing up my hair. It was full, but not eighties-hair-band full. It went down past the middle of my back. Jeanie said that guys loved long hair.

She was probably right. I saw a lot of the jocks at school running their hands through the cheerleaders' hair, and every single one of them had long hair. Huh, I hadn't realized that until today. Even Corbin's last girlfriend had long hair. But he never dated anyone for long. And they always hated me. One said he had to choose between her and me. Guess who he chose? Yup, that's right. His life-long best friend.

Sadly, though, he still referred to me as his bestie. Oh well, that just meant I would always be there, and those girls wouldn't.

"Do you think if I reminded him that we used to run around in the water naked he might think differently of me?" I had seen a movie where two kids who played together naked ended up getting together later in life. Would that work now?

Jeanie just about had a heart attack laughing so hard. "No, I wouldn't recommend it. He'd get the wrong idea."

I shrugged. "Yeah, you're probably right." Then I looked again in the mirror. "Do you really think he'll see me as all grown up? And not the little girl he played in the mud with only until a few years ago?"

When a snort escaped Jeanie, I turned to look at her. She was fixing her hair, probably from the near apoplexy from laughing so hard at me a moment ago.

She nodded. "Yes, he will. I think he's done with pulling your ponytails and throwing spitballs at you."

"Eww, did you have to remind me about the spitballs?" If he even thought about throwing a spitball at me while in this dress, I'd...well...I'd push him in the pool. That's what I'd do. "He better not be doing any of that stupid kid stuff tonight."

"It only means he's into you and doesn't know how to tell you, that's all. At least, that's what my mom told me when I first met Browning." She got this dreamy-eyed expression and looked off into the distance.

I just about gagged. Jeanie and Browning were one of those sickeningly sweet couples. They were always holding hands and kissing. They had even gotten each other pledge rings. Not the marriage ones, but the kind for staying pure. They promised each other to wait for their wedding night. But the way they looked at each other, I doubted they'd make it to graduation. They'd probably end up a statistic and do it at prom. Then she'd get preggers and they'd have to get married. I hoped that wasn't the case.

I mean, I wanted them to get married—they were too cute together, and way too much in love. They needed to marry. But the idea that they were going to wait for their wedding night was romantic. I wanted to meet a guy like that one day. One who loved me enough to wait.

Instead, I'd get asked out by other fringe guys who just wanted a quick bump in the back seat of their parents' car. No thank you!

I snapped my fingers in front of Jeanie's face. "Earth to Jeanie. Wake up, Jeanie."

"Huh?" She batted her eyelashes and smiled at me. "Okay, are we ready to go now? I hear the music playing, and there are already a lot of people in your backyard."

I felt a few drops of perspiration on my forehead, and then one large sweat bead rolled down my back. Gross. "Yup, let's show them our new dresses." I had on a designer knock-off. It was a black taffeta gown that went just below my knees. The bodice was tight and showed off what little cleavage I had, as well as my tanned arms. I had been working on my tan this past week, as well as building up my biceps over the past two months. Just in anticipation of this charity event.

My parents supported an orphanage in Africa. We'd even been there to help out with the little kids before. And tonight's event was a fundraiser. A lot of the city's social elite were going to be there, as well as a good group of rich people from O.C. And Corbin's family would be there along with a few of the parents of other football players. Thankfully, none of the cheerleaders were coming. I was grateful for that little bit of good news.

When we made it down the stairs, we mingled inside and I had a few people I had to say hi to. Mostly friends of my parents.

"Well hello, gorgeous," a sultry male voice said from behind me, and I turned, starting to smile. Then when I saw who it was, I froze. *Could it be?* "Jackson Devencourt? What you doing here? I thought you were off at NYU?"

Jackson was the son of my dad's business partner.

"I am, but Dad thought I should be here tonight. You know, to mingle with the right crowd." He grinned at me, then took a very long and slow look down my body. "And I'm very glad I did. You look amazing."

My cheeks heated and I looked down at my hands. They were fidgeting with one of the pieces of taffeta on my gown. "Thank you." Then I got my courage up and looked him the eye. Jeanie told me I was smokin' hot, and now with Jackson looking at me like he wanted to eat me up, I was gaining the courage I needed for the night. "You look very nice yourself." And I meant it. He was hot.

I'd had a crush on him ever since I started liking boys. He was my first crush, but nothing ever came of it. He was two years older than me, and he would never be interested in a fringe girl. He only dated cheerleaders.

In fact, "Hey, aren't you still dating Emily? How is she?" Emily was the head cheerleader from his senior year. They'd gotten together and were thick as thieves all through junior and senior year. I thought for sure they'd get married.

But when he was accepted into NYU and she wasn't accepted at Juilliard, it wasn't looking good. She ended up going to college in Texas; she got a full-ride for cheerleading.

A shadow crossed Jackson's features. "We aren't together any-more." It sounded as though he wasn't the one who'd made that decision.

"I'm sorry. I know you really cared for her." Not knowing what to do, I hugged him. And oh, did he smell divine. If I wasn't all about Corbin these days, Jackson would totally be my new main crush.

He wrapped his arms around me and pulled tight. When he whispered, "Thank you," into my ear, my body melted against his.

Hmm, if things with Corbin didn't go well tonight, maybe I'd get a kiss from Jackson. At least he seemed attracted to me.

Jackson pulled back and looked at me with smoldering eyes. "When did you grow up?"

The old crush was coming back, and hard.

"Say, do you want to go somewhere more private?" He leaned in and ran a hand down my arm.

Then my radar kicked off, and I realized he was just looking for someone to take Emily's place for a night. Not my cup of tea, thank you very much.

"Sorry, I can't leave. I have to mingle and talk to the guests. This is my parents' party, remember?" I pulled back and made a note to stay away from older guys. Especially ones on the rebound.

"Right, of course. Sorry about that." He waved and walked away.

Jeanie walked up to me and whispered, "What was that all about?"

"He's on the rebound and looking for a one-night stand." I snorted, wondering how in the world he could have thought I'd be into that.

Jeanie chortled. "You're better off with Corbin anyway. The two of you make such a cute couple. But"—she put a manicured finger to her lips—"you might be able to use Jackson tonight to make Corbin jealous."

"Yeah, right." I shook my head. "I doubt Corbin's going to see me as anything other than the little kid he thinks I am."

"Not in that outfit he won't. Trust me. If you got Jackson to proposition you, you look hot." Jeanie was so great for my confidence. She always knew exactly what to say.

"Alright, where is the man of the hour? Have you seen him yet?" I turned, looking at everyone else in the room we were in, then dragged Jeanie through the rest of the house. I figured Corbin would be in the kitchen or dining room eating the hors d'oeuvres.

He wasn't anywhere in the house. I should have known. If I'd thought about it, I would have realized where he would be...outside.

When we were little, he always wanted to be outside. A memory of when we were only five years old made its way up from the deep recesses of my mind. I hadn't thought about that in years. It wasn't something I wanted anyone to know about, but Corbin and I had played in the mud one summer on more than one occasion. We had an issue with faulty sprinklers one year and they kept breaking, causing various areas of our backyard to turn muddy.

When Corbin learned of it, he'd goaded me into checking it out. It didn't take much back then to get me to follow him around. I think even then I had a crush on him, but didn't realize what it was back then. To me, he was my best friend and playmate.

When we made it to the back of the yard, he dared me to run through the mess. I shook my head and then thought I had a wonderful comeback. "I dare *you* to run through the mud. If it's so fun, you do it." I could remember thinking I was so smart to turn his dare around on him. Little did I know, he was the smart one.

He grinned at me and took off without a thought. When he ran through the mess, it got all over him. I wasn't exactly a girly-girl back then, but when he ran up to me I started to scream and tried to get away from him. Instead, he chased me through the mud and I started laughing. It didn't hurt or feel gross like I thought it would.

Instead, it felt like freedom.

Freedom from the strict no-dirt rules my mom had initiated that summer.

Turned out, I was a bit of dirt collector. I rarely took my shoes off when I came inside, and the evidence of where I'd been would end up all over the house.

On this occasion, though, I knew better. Instead of tracking the mud inside, I jumped in the shallow end of the pool. Corbin followed me, and we splashed each other until the mud was off. Both of us had learned to swim that summer and thought we were so grown up and smart to clean off in the pool.

Turned out we were wrong...

My mother was furious with us both.

A small grin spread across my face as Jeanie and I walked out back. I knew exactly where Corbin would be now, and wished we were five years old again. That summer was so easy and carefree. Now that we were teenagers, everything had become so complicated. Why couldn't we go back to the silly pranks and fun we used to have?

Jeanie walked outside first and stopped in front of the door.

I stood inside waiting for her to move. "Jeanie, come on. What's the hold-up?"

"Shh, I don't see him yet." Jeanie's head turned this way and that as she waved me back into the house. "I want you to make an entrance."

I rolled my eyes and sighed. She was always so dramatic. But, also right. I needed to make a stellar entrance to catch his attention. Using Jackson to make Corbin jealous would be plan B. Maybe.

Her head bobbed up once, and she whispered over her shoulder, "He's behind the pool with a few of his football buddies. Let's walk out slowly and mingle. Take our time heading that way. You can't look like you're looking for him. And if he notices you early, he'll be wanting you to come his way. You have to keep him wanting more."

Just that week Jeanie and I had been reading an article in *Cosmo* that talked about this very thing. The way to get a man interested in you was to create desire. And to create desire, one had to be out of reach. It made no sense to me. How could a guy try to get a woman if she was out of reach? Wouldn't it make more sense to be available? This was probably why I rarely had a date. I was too available.

Being a teen was hard.

Being a woman was even harder.

Would it be this difficult when I was a grownup? I hoped not.

However, if all went well tonight then I wouldn't have to worry. Corbin would become my high-school sweetheart and we'd get married after college. Just like in my dreams.

Following along with Jeanie's plan, we walked around and chatted with my parents' guests, most of whom I really didn't know. Then we went to the refreshments table and picked up glasses of punch. Jeanie angled me just so Corbin could see my profile, and I could barely see him from out of the corner of my eye. He hadn't noticed me yet, which frustrated me.

Or if he had, I hadn't caught his eye.

"Jeanie, what do I do now?"

Her eyes darted to and fro. "Let's walk toward the pool. He won't be able to miss you if we walk directly through his line of sight. But whatever you do, *don't* look his way. Pretend as though you don't notice him."

"Got it." I put my empty glass of punch on the table and we casually strolled away. Well, it was a practiced casual. Lately Jeanie and I had been practicing different walks and looks that we saw on TV and in the glamorous magazines. It was important for us to be seen as though we knew how to carry ourselves. "Comport" was the word my mom used. Even she was happy to help us with our walks and looks.

This was it. This was the moment I had been dreaming about. Corbin would finally notice me and he'd want no one else. I'd be the center of his attention, and I'd finally have the man of my dreams. Nothing was going to mess this up.

Chapter 6

I hated the society parties, but the food was always good. I knew this party was one of those hoity-toity ones to raise money for good charities, and I didn't have any issues with that part. But having to dress up? That part sucked, big time.

The suit and tie my mother had chosen for me weren't exactly the best for throwing the pigskin around. So I had taken off the jacket and tie and was out back, behind the pool and most of the guests, throwing the football around with a couple of my teammates. This was the only way to pass the time. Well, besides sampling the food.

Okay, so there might be some cute chicks here, but they were all so uppity. Why couldn't the pretty cheerleaders be fun like Millie? And why did they have to treat her so poorly? She was my best friend, and to be honest, one of the nicest people I'd ever met. There was no reason for anyone to treat her so horribly. Her parents were part of the town's society. It wasn't like she lived on the wrong side of the tracks, like in those eighties movies everyone loved to watch.

In fact, Millie always wanted to watch the kind of movies I liked to watch—action and adventure. She never wanted to watch the sappy romance stuff that other girls gushed over. My last girlfriend refused to watch *The Fast and The Furious, Tokyo Drift*. Instead, I had to watch some sappy movie called *The Break-Up*. What a waste. I couldn't be sure, but I thought I might have fallen asleep in that one.

Okay, maybe Jennifer Aniston was hot for an old lady, but there was zero action. No car chases. No explosions. Nothing a red-blooded man wanted to see. Instead, I had to watch a show about breaking up? Really?

The very next night, Millie and I went to see *Tokyo Drift*. When it was over, we spent the next two hours talking about the different scenes in the movie and comparing it to the other *Fast and Furious* movies. That night was so much better than my date. So on Monday, I broke up with the girl. Now I was dateless and throwing a ball back and forth with my friends at a society party.

Speaking of which, where was Millie? She should be here. Her mother was probably trying to introduce her to some Harvard stiff. I chuckled when I thought about how disappointed Mrs. Milan would be when Millie snubbed the stooge. Of course the guy would be into her—she was a society daughter—but Millie wasn't anything like those stuck-up snobs who dated Ivy League guys. Which was just fine with me. If she started dating those types, she'd stop being fun and turn into one of them. Or worse, her mother. An involuntary shudder wracked my body and I almost missed the catch.

I needed a break.

I needed to find my best friend and rescue her from a boring night with a snob.

With football in hand, I turned to scan the backyard for Millie so I could rescue her.

Instead, a beauty in a black gown caught my attention, and all thoughts of my best buddy fled.

Somewhere in the hazy recesses of my brain, I knew this goddess. Then, Jake's voice interrupted and demanded I throw him the ball. Without taking my eyes off of the most beautiful woman I'd ever laid eyes on, I threw it.

Only, instead of aiming for a football player, I aimed where my eyes were focused.

Chapter 7

Millie

Fantastic, the cheer squad had shown up to my mother's party. Of course they would. Their parents were part of the same group of friends my parents were. Why oh why did I let Jeanie talk me into taking my time to cross the yard? If only I'd have made my way to Corbin five minutes earlier, then he would have noticed me. Now he'd be checking out the pretty girls in their mini-skirts and low-cut dresses.

Was that Melinda in a backless tank-style dress that barely covered her girly bits? How could her mother let her out dressed in something so risqué? Then I saw her mother and realized they both shopped at the same boutique, Nudity 'R' Us. At least my mother dressed appropriately for her age.

But then again, my mother was happily married. If I wasn't mistaken, Melinda's parents were divorced. I think her dad was living with their former nanny? Or something just as scandalous. The woman couldn't be older than twenty-two. A part of me felt sorry for Melinda. That was until I saw Corbin eyeing her.

Then a football came straight at my chest.

It hit me so hard, I fell back into the pool. I swear, my short-lived life flashed before my eyes and I realized I hadn't even started living yet. How could I die so young? Sure, my body would forever be remembered as young and pretty, but I'd never get to see if Corbin thought I was a pretty woman, ever.

Why oh why was life so unfair?

I spluttered as my head popped above water. Thankfully, I was a good swimmer. Sadly, I'd worn the wrong dress for a swim. The layers, now soaked through, were trying to pull me down to the depths of the nine-foot pool.

Maybe I should just go with what the world was telling me. It was time I disappeared.

Instead, my arms worked on auto-pilot to bring myself back up. Then I thought that if I could get more air, I could make my way to the side of the pool where I knew adults would help me up. I was still a helpless child in most of their eyes, wasn't I? Or did they ignore me like Corbin?

Someone's strong arms wrapped around me and pulled me back up to the surface. "I'm so sorry, I can't believe I did that to you." A voice I'd recognize anywhere, even in this situation—Corbin.

I realized as I flailed about, trying not to drag us both down to our deaths, he was attempting to rescue me. Although he deserved to die, I didn't want him to perish like this.

I'd have to survive so I could plan his death. Something slow and painful.

Now that I knew I wasn't going to drown in my own pool in front of the most popular kids at school, I was embarrassed.

Corbin pulled me to the side and proceeded to tear off the bottom of my dress as I held onto the side for dear life. My dress that cost over four hundred dollars. Never mind that the chlorine from the pool had already destroyed it, how dare he rip my dress apart in front of everyone?

Two sets of strong arms reached down and pulled me up while I struggled to drop back down in the water so no one could see my legs.

"Dude, that was classic!" Jake joked. His were one set of arms helping me out.

"Perfect shot!" said the other arms. Those belonged to Armando, another football player.

And behind them, the catty girls of the cheer squad were laughing and pointing at me.

Great, I was going to be the joke of the entire school. And school hadn't even started yet.

The moment I was up and away from the edge of the pool, I turned fiery eyes on Corbin. "I never want to see you again!" I turned and stormed off to my room with Jeanie in tow.

I never did.

Chapter 8

Millie
Present Day

Thoughts of the last time I'd actually spoken to Corbin fluttered through my memory. I had worked for years to shut those memories away, never to be considered again. Until today. Of course he would be present for another major disaster and embarrassment. It was all I could do to keep from wanting to crawl away and hide for the rest of summer, just like I did that summer before my senior year.

After doing the best I could with what was available to me, I walked back out to the tiny security office where two police officers were reviewing a video of the worst moment of my adult life. Great, now the entire precinct would watch this. They'd probably play it back while they sat there drinking coffee and eating donuts. And I'd be stuck in a jail cell, still mostly covered in mud, and probably suffering from a spider bite. Could I die from the bite? That might be just the ticket.

Then they'd all feel so guilty for laughing at me and not letting me clean up.

Although, with my luck I'd probably rot in the cell for days before anyone noticed the smell. Thanks to my dip in the mud, I doubted I'd smell any worse for quite some time.

When I walked into the room, one of the officers turned around and grimaced. "You took quite a fall. Are you alright?" The elderly cop turned worried eyes on me.

Finally, someone who actually cared about what had happened to me. Hopefully he'd hear me out before arresting me. "I'm sore and filthy. I think a hot bath—or three—and some rest will be all I need."

I noticed a chair and went to sit in it.

The security guard pulled it back before I could sit down and I almost fell on my backside. When I looked up to see who had grabbed me from under my arms, I wished I had fallen.

Fierce green eyes stared at me. "Jeez, Millie. What's happened to you?"

"Oh, this is my fault?" I tried to straighten my clothes as best I could. When I looked around, I noticed the security guard sheepishly holding the chair I was trying to sit in. I pointed at him. "He pulled the chair out from under me, literally." I glared at the boy and wished I had never set foot in this mall. I knew I never would again.

"Sorry ma'am, but you're all dirty. And this is my only chair." He shrugged.

The nice police officer cleared his throat. "Miss?"

"Millie Milan. Well, Millicent Milan is my full name." I sighed. Here it came—he was going to arrest me on shoplifting charges and I'd have a permanent stain on what had once been a spotless record. Shoot, I even had a credit score of over eight hundred, for pity's sake.

Not many could boast about that kind of score these days. But that would probably go down too, now that I'd be a jailbird.

"Miss Milan, I think we can clear this up easily. I saw that you didn't actually leave the store of your own free will."

The other cop sniggered and put a hand over his mouth while his eyes went back to the video. The stupid security guard was replaying the most embarrassing moment of my life and that cop was watching, again.

"Thank you, Officer…" I looked at his badge and continued, "Officer Baily. I never would have walked out with the purse without paying for it."

"Yes, well." Officer Baily cleared his throat and tried hard to avert his gaze from the screens showing my fall from grace. "I think if you could just pay for the bag, I could get the store manager to forget all about it."

I drooped with relief. Finally, someone was on my side. "Yes, I told the rent-a-cop here"—I pointed to Barney Fife—"that I'd be happy to pay for the purse, since it was damaged in my fall. But he refused my offer." I glared at the boy, who shrank back.

"It wasn't my decision to make. I had already phoned the police when you made that offer." He turned toward Officer Baily. "She only made the offer after she was caught. I know her type—she would have walked away and never said a word."

"You're wrong." The voice who stood up for me shocked me, again. Corbin went on to tell them all what a stand-up and honest person I was. "Millie would never steal a thing. She has no need to steal. Besides, if you knew her you'd know she's one of the most generous people around." He glared at the mall cop.

Since I hadn't said more than two words to him since that fateful pool party, I had no idea he knew anything about my life. But here he was telling them about the various charity organizations I was a part of.

Had Corbin stalked me?

"Look, Deputy Fife." Now Corbin was reading my mind and calling this little punk the same name I had dubbed him in my head? What was going on here? Maybe this was a dream. Or a nightmare. "If you would have just watched the video and used that little pea brain of yours, you would have seen this was all an accident. I witnessed it. And I can tell you that there's no way Millie would have fallen into the mud just to steal a fifty-dollar purse."

The security guard crossed his scrawny arms over his chest. Then defiantly said, "how do you know?"

"Because I've known Millie Milan since we were little kids." Corbin glared at the kid, towering over him. While Corbin was at least six feet tall, Mark couldn't have been more than five feet, six inches tall.

Even I was taller than this kid, without heels. In fact, he was the shortest person in the room. The only one smaller than him was Bella. And she was a dog.

Mark spluttered and took a step toward the other cop, the one who'd laughed at me. "Officer Martin, do you agree with this hare-brained idea?"

Officer Martin had been leaning over the counter, replaying the video over and over. He had stopped laughing on the third or fourth replay and instead was focused on the beginning of the tape. "Yes, actually I do. I can see here from the replay that Mille is only guilty of being unlucky. She had been walking out when something caught her eye. She stopped next to the door and picked up the purse. Before she could put it down, she was being assaulted by the mob in the store."

The cop stood up, and I just about gulped. He was the tallest in the room. This giant of a cop stood well over six feet. Probably closer to six feet five inches. I wondered if he'd played basketball in high school, then quickly shoved that thought aside and paid attention again.

"If you would have done your job, those women would have been under control much sooner and Miss Milan would never have been shoved out of the store." Officer Martin eyed the room and snorted. "Of course, you were in here eating donuts and watching the monitors, weren't you?" It wasn't a question. The cop narrowed his eyes and waited for Mark to confess all.

Before Mark could say a word, Officer Baily interjected, "I bet you were watching the baseball game instead of the mall cameras." He narrowed his eyes. "You should have picked up on the chaos that's out there much sooner."

Mark shrank into himself and backed up against the wall. "Yes, I confess," he moaned. "I didn't even notice the issues until the manager of the dress shop called." Then he realized what was happening and got down on his knees. "Please don't tell the mall manager. I'll lose my job."

The cops both shook their heads.

"You shouldn't be here all alone when it's this crazy, anyways. Go back outside and try to get people back in line. And next time, just let a lady pay for the merchandise when she so obviously didn't shoplift." Officer Baily pulled his radio closer to his mouth and called in to his precinct.

I couldn't understand half of what he'd said; most of it was in cop-code. And I really didn't care. All that mattered was my name wasn't mentioned. As he finished his call, I pulled out my wallet and got the cash out. All I wanted to do was pay for the purse and get home. I handed the cop three twenties and said, "Tell the dress shop manager to keep the change." I didn't care about a few dollars, and I certainly wouldn't be coming back here to get my change, ever.

Corbin insisted on walking me out. The moment we were away from the security office, and the insufferable fool who thought he was more TJ Hooker than Barney Fife, I turned to Corbin. Was that a twinge or a flutter in my stomach? I couldn't be sure what I was feeling, other than embarrassment.

Embarrassment over how I looked, but also over the fact that Corbin Deeks had to defend my honor to two cops and a jerk of a rent-a-cop who was barely out of puberty. It was all so humiliating.

"Corbin, thank you for your help." I sighed, not knowing what else to say. Instead of prolonging this goodbye, for surely he'd be just as interested in getting away from me as I was away from him, I gave him a tiny small and small wave.

"Wait," Corbin called out. "It was good seeing you again." He snorted and shook his head. "Well, the situation was odd, but I've wanted to talk to you forever."

I held up my hand. "Thank you, but I really need to get home and hosed off before this all sticks to my body forever. Whoever thought a mud bath was a good thing has never actually been in the mud before."

A wry smile crossed his lips. "Still as effervescent as ever, I see. Well, I'd like to talk sometime, when you're feeling up to the challenge."

Up to the challenge? What did he think this was, the fourth grade? Did he think a double-dare would get me to talk to him? I took a deep, calming breath and considered the situation from his end and relented. "I'll see you around, Corbin."

After what felt like years, but really wasn't even two hours, I was home and in the shower. Not only was I going to have to get my car detailed, but I would have to answer to the lady who cleaned my house. I tried, really I did, but I couldn't get all of the mud out of the grout between the tiles.

With my luck, I'd have to get someone in here to replace the grout, and probably the tile, after all was said and done.

Thankfully, I kept a blanket in my car so I'd sat on that as I drove home. But the dried mud flaked off my body with every tiny movement and by the time I got home, the interior was filthy. I didn't even bother trying to clean the blanket. With everything else I had to deal with, I just threw it directly into the trash bin. It was an old blanket anyway.

Now, three hours later, I was sitting in front of my TV watching an old movie on A&E. Stupid Hallmark was all about Christmas, again. At this point, I never wanted to see another cherub or sprig of mistletoe again. And don't get me started on the Christmas lights. Argh.

Instead, I was watching a very old rendition of Jane Austen's *Persuasion*. This was exactly what I needed. An old, almost Gothic-style movie. It fit my mood perfectly. I had forgotten that Alice Krige starred in this one. I loved her as the Borg queen. Both actresses who played the Borg Queen were great, but Alice was my favorite. Actually, I loved everything she'd ever done. Maybe I'd do a themed month of my own and make it all about Alice Krige, or *Star Trek*. Or both? Yeah, that'd be the ticket.

And I might sneak in another Jane Austen movie here and there. The classics always got me in a good mood.

Chapter 9

Corbin

Seeing Millie again brought up so many memories. My mother had done a good job keeping me informed as to what my old pal had been up to since high school. I missed her. Man, I still felt horrible about what happened the summer before our senior year.

Today's mishap only served to remind me how badly I'd screwed up. Poor Millie, she never recovered her social standing after that party. The cheerleaders never missed a chance to bring it up, either. And where were they now? Most of them were divorced or in loveless marriages. Millie had gone on to be quite successful in her career, if my mother was to be believed. And I was sure she was right. Our parents were still great friends.

I tried for a year to repair our friendship. I sent her flowers, chocolate, and letters. Lots of letters. But she never forgave me. I couldn't blame her. Maybe if the mean girls hadn't been there it would have been alright, but they were. And what a waste. I still had the vision of Millie in that black dress in my head.

And there went my heart, again. Every time I thought about her in her backyard at the pool party, my heart went crazy. Every fantasy I've had of her since then has starred her in that sexy black dress.

She's still the most beautiful woman I've ever met. I could tell, even with the mud and all that mess, she was stunning. And she liked Bella. She must have visited my parents whenever I was out of town because Bella seemed to know her as well.

If only I could find a way to see her again. Over the years my parents tried getting us together, even her parents did. But every time we ended up in the same place, she'd leave.

I took a seat on my sofa, trying to come up with a way to get near Millie again. Now that we were adults, maybe she'd hear me out? It had been fourteen years since the incident—surely she'd be over it by now? Then again, I did see her do a facer in the mud today. Yesterday, she might have been open to talking to me. But after today? Highly doubtful.

Bella jumped up on the sofa next to me.

"You'll never turn your back on me, will you?" I leaned down and my little dog licked my face. "Yup, you're my faithful friend. You'll always be here, won't you, girl?" I scratched behind her ears and we got comfortable on the couch as I turned on an old movie. *Die Hard*. Now that's a Christmas movie.

Once the movie was over, I flipped the channels until I landed on the news. When I jumped up it scared poor Bella, who barked and jumped down on the ground.

"Oh, no. She's never going to forgive me." I rubbed my hand down my face. "But to be fair, Bella, this wasn't my fault. I had nothing to do with this. I was only a witness, nothing more."

Bella jumped back on the couch and I took my seat as I watched in horror while the news anchor dubbed the fiasco the "Christmas Horde Stampede." A video of what happened to Millie today flashed before my eyes and I prayed no one we knew was watching, all the while knowing that someone would see it and word would spread.

Poor Millie. The camera angles showing her fall right into the mud didn't come from what I had seen in the security office. Which meant that either someone had been filming on their cell phone... Oh no. I watched in horror as I realized this was only a recap. The whole story had been played earlier on the five o'clock news. Our entire extended group of acquaintances would have seen this. Poor Millie.

I looked at the clock and knew it was too late to call, but didn't care. I had to know what was being done to help my old friend.

"Mom? Did you see?" I asked when my mother picked up on the first ring. Normally she and Dad went to bed early, but they must have been out at an event or party tonight if she was still up. It was almost eleven o'clock.

"Yes, we've been discussing what can be done to help her. Why didn't you call me earlier, after you got home? I saw in the news report that you were there when it all went down. Did she finally talk to you?"

I sighed. I didn't want to go into the entire story. The fact that the cops had been called just for her wasn't part of the news story, and I had no plans to share that juicy bit of gossip with anyone. Not even my parents. "Not really. I just happened to be there when she fell. It was a coincidence, that's all."

"So, are you two on talking terms again, then?" my mother asked.

"No. While she did have a few things to say to me, I doubt she'll ever talk to me again. Not after today. I saw her fall in the mud. Now that it's all over the news, she'll probably move away for good. Knowing her, she might even feel she has to move halfway around the world to escape this." I hoped that wasn't the case, but this was Millie we were talking about.

If she'd had her way, she would have gone to a boarding school for her senior year. Or at least, that's what my mother had told me she wanted to do. But her parents refused.

"I'm sorry, sweetie. I know you've always wanted to re-establish that friendship. Honestly, I don't know what's wrong with that girl. All you ever did was look out for her. If not for you, she never would have had a social life."

My mom meant well, but she was wrong.

I learned in my senior year that the reason Millie had such a hard time socially was because of me. The popular girls all wanted me and thought Millie was in their way. I wasn't exaggerating. After senior year started, they swarmed me and tried to get in my good graces. When they weren't making fun of Millie, they were ignoring her and hanging all over my every word.

Jake told me right before prom that he overheard Melinda complaining that Millie was still in their way. I never went to senior prom. I tried asking Millie to be my date, but she never responded. And I didn't want to go with any of those clingy chicks. I never regretted staying home and having a *Die Hard* marathon followed by a string of various James Bond movies. I gotta say, no one was better than Sean Connery as agent 007.

"Mom, let's not discuss the past. What I want to know is how we can help her now. I don't want her to scurry back into her shell again. From everything you and Mrs. Milan have said, she's flourished over the past decade. I'd hate to see her lose that joy she found." I had seen pictures of Millie and she was even more gorgeous than in high school.

She had taken over her parents' charity work and went to Africa at least once a year to help the program her parents were a part of.

She actually worked hand in hand with the poor women, teaching them how to start their own online business and market it. Millie helped women become financially independent. And unlike others who made a big deal out of their charitable acts, she kept her work quiet. She didn't want any praise for what she did. All she wanted was for those women to live better lives.

The woman blossomed. If only I'd seen her as more than my childhood friend sooner, maybe I wouldn't have thrown that football at her when she wore that black dress to the party. Ugh, thinking of that moment has always caused a huge pain in my chest. That was the worst day of my entire life.

I was so overcome with shock and attraction that I didn't even know what I was doing until it was too late. Of course, I was the only one who would jump in and save her. Not that she needed saving; my Millie was a fantastic swimmer. But, that dress...I was sure it would weigh her down, and I couldn't take the chance that she'd struggle to get her head above water.

Regret still lay heavily over every memory from that night.

Even now, I realized my fist was rubbing my chest. I think a hole had opened up and my heart had been yanked out. But what could I do? She wouldn't talk to me before today, and I could still see the glare she'd given me when she left the mall. If looks could kill...

"Well, I suppose we could make sure we squelch any discussions of her and today's incident as we hear them." My mom always had great ideas when it came to this sort of thing.

"Anything I can do?" Even though it wasn't my fault at all, I still wanted to help where I could. I wanted her back in my life. No, scratch that, I needed her back in my life.

Part of the reason I took that job in Orange County all those years ago was to get away from Millie, or at least from the idea that I'd see her around town, and it hurt too much to know that she would ignore me. Treat me as though I were a total stranger. Or worse, see her out on a date with someone else.

I kept rehashing the way she'd looked at me when she left and felt as though there was nothing I could do to get back in her good graces.

"I have it!" my mother exclaimed. I had to pull the phone away from my ears. She had never screamed over the phone, as far as I could remember.

When the phone went dead, I worried I'd lost her. "Mother? Are you there?"

"Yes, yes. Leave it all up to me. And dear, you won't be coming to the Milans' party this weekend."

"What? I've been uninvited?"

"No, no. The Milans want you there, but I'm uninviting you. At least for the moment. I'll give Evelyn your regrets that a last-minute project has come up and you have to work Saturday."

"But Mom, I don't have to work." This was getting out of hand. I needed to be there to see how Millie was doing and see if I could finally get her to talk to me, again. "I want to be there for Millie. She's going to need more support after all of this."

"Exactly. But she won't attend if she thinks you're there." My mom paused a moment. "Think about it, dear."

Then it hit me. "Good idea, Mother."

Chapter 10

Millie

Done, totally done. I was never going anywhere ever again. It was bad enough that those cops and Corbin knew what happened. But the news? How in the world was I prime-time news? This made no sense whatsoever.

And now I was going to lose my job. I just knew it. For who in their right mind would want a marketing manager that was just splashed all over the local news? For all I knew, the networks would pick it up and it would go viral. ABC Designs, the company I worked for, wouldn't want someone who did a facer in the mud during a Christmas-Crazy riot.

That stupid news anchor made it sound as though I was the one who started it all, too! That's crazy—Christmas Crazy. Just one more reason to stay home for the entirety of the summer. Not for my health like last year, but for my own sanity.

Everywhere I turned, it was "Merry Christmas" this or "Merry Christmas" that. No one was even using "season's greetings" anymore.

But to be fair there weren't any other holidays—except for the Fourth of July, which was only celebrated in the US—for the world to offer greetings to.

It was strange. In the past, I always hated it when people said, "season's greetings." For it was the Christmas season. Sure, I knew other holidays were celebrated during those two months. But the vast majority of the world, and the US, celebrated Christmas. So why couldn't we say, "Merry Christmas?" It had become politically incorrect to say it. Now it was all of a sudden PC to use the word "Christmas," and I hated it.

What was wrong with me?

This was exactly what I wanted only two years ago—for everyone to remember what we were celebrating.

Or was something wrong with the world?

I sighed and turned off my TV. I didn't need to be reminded of what I looked like with my face in the mud and clumps of the brown stuff all down the front of my now-trashed outfit. If it wasn't so hot, I would have burned it in my fireplace. But there was no way I was going to start a fire when it was still over eighty degrees outside at night.

"This is going to be the worst summer since I was seventeen. If only I had a dog to keep me company, and to talk to." I was sure if anyone was watching, they'd say I'd gone off my rocker. Talking out loud to oneself, even when no one else is around, is very much frowned upon. If only I had a country estate to run away to, like the heroines in those regency books I loved to read. Then I'd end up meeting a earl or a duke who was also in hiding, and we'd live happily ever after.

Happily ever after? "Pft, yeah right. Like that's ever going to happen to me."

I picked up the teddy bear on my lounge chair and decided he would do. "Teddy, is it better to be caught talking to a stuffed animal than myself? Because I think you and I are going to be the only ones who will want to be around us for quite some time."

The next morning I decided I'd work from home. Thankfully I had the sort of schedule that allowed me to work from home part-time and in the office part-time. Work was exactly what I needed to keep my mind off of everything.

When my cell phone rang, I sighed. It was lunchtime, and that could only mean one person: my mother. "Hi Mom." I saw her name on the caller ID when I answered.

"Millie, dear. What are you going to do about the news report?" She was nothing if not straight to the point today. Normally she hemmed and hawed a bit before trying to sidestep issues. This was new.

Unless she was super worried about me. Then all bets were off. If my mother, who was the center of the gossip circles around town, was worried for my reputation, then it was bad.

"Is it that bad?" I cringed, knowing it was, but I still needed to hear it from her.

A crackle went through the line, and I wondered if we'd lost connection before she spoke up. "Dear, I think we need to have a pow-wow. Why don't you come over for dinner tonight and we can discuss how best to handle this?"

It wasn't exactly an order, but she really didn't ask, either. However, she was one of the best people I knew to discuss how to get out of a rotten situation like what I was in. And my father could help as well.

Between the two of them, they'd know what to do and who to enlist in whatever schemes they came up with.

So it was with that thought in mind that I walked into my parents' house later that night. Worry didn't even come close to what went through my body when I saw who all was sitting in their formal living room. Mr. and Mrs. Deeks sat there with iced tea in their hands, smiling at me as shock filled my body.

My head turned, looking everywhere, and I could have sworn it would have fallen off if *he* had been there, too. If my doctor was there right then taking my blood pressure, I bet he'd have admitted me to the hospital. My blood was pumping a zillion miles a minute. The rushing sound and the beats from my heart were all I could hear.

Thank the good Lord, but Corbin wasn't anywhere in sight. That didn't mean he wasn't invited, it just meant that he wasn't present—for the moment.

"Mom, Dad, you didn't tell me you had invited others. I would have dressed nicer." Since I had thought it would be just the three of us, I was wearing white capris, a Hawaiian-print blouse, and pink sandals. It had been a hot day, and my parents didn't exactly set the A/C where I liked it. Not that they were cheapskates, but well, they were old. Like really old. The kind of old who grew up without A/C in their homes, I think.

Okay, so they weren't ancient, but let's get real, most older people liked it hotter than those of us who were younger. I don't know why, but they seemed to think that keeping the house at seventy-eight was smart. Me? I liked it at seventy-two. Then when I went to bed at night, I turned it down even lower—sixty-eight.

So whenever I went to their house on a hot day, I dressed for the heat. Besides, they had a fantastic backyard that always had an evening breeze. Which was where we normally ate our dinner and sat around for a while talking. If it was cool enough, they even turned off the A/C and opened the windows to get the cooler air coming over the Santa Ana Mountains from Orange County and the breeze that always came in off the ocean.

Okay, okay, I kinda liked it on those nights. I didn't know what was wrong with me, but everything was setting me off lately. Normally I was pretty laid back and loved the Deeks. It was always nice when they joined us for dinner. But right now, I was in panic mode. The fact that they most likely knew all about the Christmas Crazy fiasco rankled my nerves. All I wanted was a nice, quiet dinner. One where my parents had all the answers and life went back to normal.

Even if they told me I had to date an Ivy League son of one of their country club friends, I'd probably go for that. Anything at this point to get me out of the mess I was in.

Stupid me, I'd had to go and look at social media this afternoon.

I tell you, never, and I mean never, look at social media after you've made a fool of yourself on the news. It went viral. Someone had taken the part that showed my horrified face right before it planted in the mud, sped it up through the face-plant, and then showed my face as it came up, but slowly. The mud as it dripped off my face and mouth in slow motion would have been funny if it were a cartoon. But it wasn't. It was me.

That one post alone had over a million views. I'd looked at the first two comments and turned off my phone. I couldn't do it anymore. Calling me an idiot, okay, fine. But the coarse words used were not fine. Why couldn't people be nice on social media? They had no clue what happened. All they saw was an edited version shown in such a way as to make me look like a fool, which I was for going out in that mess to begin with.

Did the world not realize that I already knew what a bad decision that was? Geesh.

And now, the parents of the one man whose opinion really mattered to me were sitting in my parents' house giving me looks of pity.

Forgot about Calgon taking me away. Where was Doc Brown and a DeLorean when I needed one? If I could go back in time, I'd tell myself to take the next two months off and hide away in a cabin. Somewhere deep in the woods where no one could find me, except for maybe bears.

That actually sounded like the perfect antidote to this situation. Hiding away from all of society until they moved on and forgot all about me would be perfect. Wouldn't it?

"Honey, you look beautiful. Don't worry about it." Mrs. Deeks stood up and walked toward me for one of those high-society air kisses. I'd known this woman since I was in diapers—you'd think that by now she would be normal and give me a hug, wouldn't you?

After the obligatory air kisses and hellos, I sat down on a chair with an overstuffed bottom cushion but very uncomfortable arms. Just in case the Deeks had been on Mars and only just arrived home moments before I arrived and didn't know my utter humiliation, I stayed quiet. If they knew what was going on, they would say something.

"Dear, I've asked the Deeks to come over tonight to help us plan how to get you off the news and back into society without a scandal." Of course I was a scandal to my mom, not her daughter who needed help with a tiny issue. No, to her it was a scandal.

Who was I kidding? Of course it was a scandal. I still thanked God that no one had said anything about the attempted robbery of that handbag. I did pay for it, so technically I didn't end up stealing anything before I left the mall. Right? Did it work that way?

"Actually, I have a great idea." I wasn't beaming, but I did start to feel a bit of joy bubble up. Or was that gastrointestinal acid going up my esophagus? I might need some Tums.

The taste in my mouth was a bit acidic. I reached down and took a long drink of the iced tea my mother set before me. It wasn't a Long Island iced tea, but in this case, it was probably better I didn't have any alcohol. Since I rarely tasted anything with alcohol in it, other than those fancy chocolates, I probably wouldn't be able to hold even one sip of a fancy drink like that. Instead I sighed and sat back, waiting for everyone to ask me what my idea was.

"Well?" my dad finally asked.

My mom and Mrs. Deeks probably knew I was being dramatic, and they didn't want to encourage me.

"I thought I'd take some time off from work and go hibernate in a cabin. Maybe even leave the state." I put a finger to my chin. "I've always wanted to see what it's like in Wyoming. Maybe I should rent a cabin out in the middle of nowhere. You know, the kind of place where they have to air-lift supplies in?"

Actually, the more I thought about it, the more fun it sounded. Maybe I could even write a book. Or an exposé on someone else while I was away. That would be one way to get attention off of me and onto someone else, right? Oh wait, if it was really good, then as an author I'd get attention. And the more attention I received, the faster everyone would *remember*, instead of forget, this Christmas Crazy in July debacle.

Chapter 11

Millie

Turns out running away was *not* what my parents or their best friends had in mind for me.

In fact, it was just the opposite...

"Sweetie." My mother gave me a condescending look, and I cringed. "I think you need to fight back. Show how strong you are. And don't let anyone bully you."

Bully me? Why, they'd been doing that ever since high school and the popular girls wanted my best friend as their boyfriend.

That was exactly why I had gone all the way to the other side of the country for college. I needed to get away from them all. Start over. And I did. I attended Bates College in Lewiston, Maine. Talk about getting away from it all. Their version of LA was very different from the California LA. In fact, I ended up learning to axe-throw while I was in Maine. Not a typical sporting event in California, but one that was a lot of fun. And a great topic at company picnics.

My time at college in Maine was what helped me get past all of the bullying I went through in high school, and attempt to forget about Corbin. I never really forgot about him, but I did find a way to box him away in my memory. At least until I came home and saw his parents. One time I even saw him from a distance.

Okay, okay, I'll admit, I was a chicken. It took my entire four years away to build up any sort of halfway decent self-value. I found a place where I fit in and had lots of friends. People who actually wanted to be near me for, well, me. Not because they wanted to impress my parents, or because they hoped they could get Corbin's attention.

Other than Jeanie, I really didn't have any friends at school. There were other people I occasionally hung out with, but I wouldn't call them friends. In fact, at our ten-year high school reunion, none of them remembered me. After that fiasco, I decided reunions were over-rated.

If only I would have stayed back there after graduation. Instead, I let my parents help me find a job close to home. Don't get me wrong, I love my parents with every fiber of my being, but they'd never truly stopped trying to get me and Corbin back together. And that wasn't going to happen. Especially now.

Maybe in another year or so when I got my next promotion, or did something spectacular, I'd have had the courage to face him again. But after yesterday? I doubted I'd ever have enough gumption to even look him in the eyes, let alone speak a word to him.

I still felt so totally and absolutely humiliated. How could God, or the universe, give me such rotten luck? The two most embarrassing moments of my life were witnessed by the one person who knew me the best, and whom I wanted to impress more than anyone else.

Life wasn't fair.

Life was cruel.

Life was... Well, it sucked.

Especially right now.

I had tuned out what they were all saying once they started talking over each other. Mrs. Deeks and my mom had apparently worked together on what I should do to fix my situation. And it was the exact opposite of what I wanted to do.

"Millie, are you paying attention?" My mom cocked her head to the side and pursed her lips.

With a huge sigh, I nodded. "Yes, Mom. But I don't know if I can do what you suggest. Won't it cause more talk?"

"It might, but only for a day or two. Then people will realize that what happened wasn't really that big of a deal. Especially when they see you interacting with everyone as though nothing at all happened." The expression on my mother's face fascinated me. Here she was talking about my future in our small circle, and she looked bored. How could she appear so uninterested and yet be totally worried about me?

"Your mother is right, Millie. I think if we parade you about town, attend all of the Christmas parties, and ignore what happened and any discussion of it, then people will either forget, or..."

Mr. Deeks interrupted. "My favorite part is where they will most likely think they remembered it all wrong. They might even think it was someone else."

My mouth opened and hung there like a limp fish.

"Dear, it's very unbecoming for a lady to gawk like that." My mother nodded at my face.

She was right; I knew better than to open my mouth like that. But, Jiminy Cricket. How could anyone think they'd remembered it wrong with the social media posts showing my face over and over at the beginning of the fall?

When I tried to point out that fact, all my dad could say was, "Photoshop."

My mom put a hand on my father's and nodded. "In this day and age, we all know that cyber-bullies love to use Photoshop and put other people's heads on different bodies."

Mrs. Deeks interjected, "Remember the one that went around with the super model's body and poor Myron's head on it?"

"That was totally obvious it wasn't Myron." He was a neighbor kid I used to know. He moved away after I returned from college. I think he actually founded an internet startup and sold out for close to a billion dollars. Last I heard, he had married a supermodel and they were living somewhere in the Mediterranean. "Hey, that's not a bad idea. I could call up Myron and go visit. I'm sure he and his wife wouldn't mind me staying for a few days, or months." I shrugged. Running was still my favorite idea.

"Honey, that's not the answer. Call Myron, maybe he could use your skills to help him with his next startup, but don't run. I hate it when you leave us." My dad, always the sweet one. Of course he wouldn't want me to leave. I was an only child and the apple of his eye.

Growing up, we played catch. My mom was never able to have another kid, and he had wanted a boy. What father didn't? But he was always happy to play with me.

"Thanks, Dad. I love you too. But I don't know if I can do this." I really didn't want to admit to hating this Christmas in July craziness. It was bad enough before the fiasco, but now? I was going to be known as the Grinch. But my heart wasn't three sizes too small. It was scorched from pain, and there wasn't anything that could heal my heart at this point.

Normally I was the one who coordinated the ugly Christmas sweater parties, or talked about heading up to the mountains for a sleigh-bell party. All used to be merry and bright, but not this year. No, this year I was the Grinch who stole Christmas. Or at least, I wanted to steal it away.

Hide it until next year, maybe?

Whoever I was now wasn't who I was normally. The world had gone crazy, even before that stupid celebrity suggested Christmas in July. Now, I had to find a way through this and back to normal. But how did one go about getting back to normal?

"We have a plan." Four of the scariest words to ever come out of my father's mouth.

My head did a face-plant into my palm. "What, pray tell, have you come up with?" I knew enough about my parents and their friends to know that they had come up with something they *thought* would be foolproof. I really did want out of this mess. I wanted to be the happy-go-lucky version of me I had been for the past nine years.

I had graduated college almost a decade ago, and life had been good. I mean really good for me. Thoughts of finding a husband had even begun swirling through my head. My career was on track, and if this week hadn't happened, I'd probably be only a year away from making vice president.

My company had kept me on when the pandemic hit and I'd stepped up in a big way, showing what I could do for them. And in return, they promoted me to marketing manager. There was only one person above me, and he didn't seem like he wanted the VP job. He dreamed of moving away to Miami, where his latest lady love lived. Which meant that when the current VP retired in the next year or two, I would be in line for his job.

Now? I'd be lucky to get a job as a barista. And if they did background checks, then I'd be screwed.

So I didn't have much of a choice. It was either sell my condo and move back in with my parents for the rest of my life, or try their plan.

"There are a lot of society events this summer, all for Christmas in July. You love Christmas, right?" Mrs. Deeks obviously didn't know I had boycotted Christmas in July.

"Normally, yes." I'd leave it at that. No need to go into my recent grinchy thoughts.

"Then you need to attend every event." My mom held up her hand when she saw my mouth begin to open to disagree. "Millie, this is important. The more you're seen out and about and happy, the less people will remember that unbecoming view of you in the mud." She arched an imperious brow, and I knew there was no way I could argue with her.

I gulped. There had to be more to it; they wouldn't have me going solo to these events. No way. They'd find a way to get me dates to each and every party, event, or outing. "No dates."

Mom's nostrils flared and her lips flattened.

I was right, she had made plans for me to have dates for these events, I was sure of it. She was nothing if not predictable. My parents wanted grandchildren. The very day I arrived home from college, they'd started planning.

I had successfully dodged every attempt at set-ups, usually because they agreed that I needed to get myself established in my career before getting married and having kids. But the year I turned thirty, they started hassling me again.

I was only thirty-one. It wasn't like it used to be—women were waiting until their late thirties to have kids now and everything worked out just fine.

"Honey, I'm not trying to get you married off, although now that I think about it, that's not a bad idea." My mother's eyes narrowed as she looked at me.

Mrs. Deeks clapped her hands, and her husband chuckled. "That's perfect. Millie, if you announced an engagement and then planned the wedding of the century—one fit for a princess—no one would even remember what happened at all. Everyone would be focused on the new couple and the wedding."

Where to begin? I hadn't dated a single man in several years. And I stress the word single, because the last two men I went out on dates with hid the fact that they were married. It wasn't until I googled them that I found out they both had families. Families who looked happy. What was with men these days? Why did they need to lie to women and get their hopes up?

I pursed my lips. My parents knew about Stew, but not about Marcus. One married man was enough for my parents to deal with. Thankfully, neither of them was anywhere near our social circles. Although, if they were in our area I would have known they were married before they could even smile at me.

"Mom, I appreciate that you want grandkids. But now isn't the time for this." It was all I could do keep my emotions in check.

Mrs. Deeks waved a hand in front of her face. "Millie's right, Evelyn. One man won't do it. She needs to be seen with various men. Make her so irresistible that all of the single men in town will defend her. Even those she isn't dating."

"Oh, I like where you're going with this, Anna." My mom and Mrs. Deeks giggled like schoolgirls and the two of them chattered back and forth in half-finished sentences that only they understood.

I looked to my dad, who rolled his eyes.

He held up his hands. "Only God knows how they understand each other."

"You really think getting a few guys to take me out will help?" If they were nice to me, it might do wonders for my self-confidence. But for my image? I doubted it.

"Just you wait and see, dear. I'll take care of everything, starting with my Christmas in July pool party. Anna and I will find you the very best single men to escort you to all of the events this summer."

If only it were that simple...

Chapter 12

Corbin

Today was the day of the party. My mom told me to act like I wasn't going, but no one even asked me if I was going. I already had my new Hawaiian-print shirt. I decided to wear the red shirt with a Santa Claus wearing that ridiculous old-fashioned swimsuit that looked more like a candy cane. And he was hangin' ten, which was what I wanted to be doing.

Anything would have been better than being the only one who thought it was supposed to be an ugly Christmas shirt party. Honestly, why was everyone wearing their best summer party clothes? Not a single person was in shorts or khakis. All the men were wearing nice Chinos or slacks while the women had on pretty summer dresses. Not a single one was Hawaiian- or Christmas-themed.

So, I stood out like a sore thumb. But that really didn't matter much—it wasn't my social standing that needed a boost. And I would most likely not get to talk to Millie, whose attention was all I was interested in today.

Last night, I actually prayed that Melinda wasn't invited. I hated it when she fawned all over me. Maybe she needed to take a spill in the pool this time? I chuckled when the image of the woman who thought she was Miss Perfect, and who would have a heart attack if even one single hair was out of place, fell into the pool. She'd probably have a stroke if she fell in.

Too bad I couldn't make that happen without feeling guilty.

Oh well. If God wanted it to happen, it would. Or something else would come along to take any unwanted attention away from Millie.

I decided I'd make the rounds and see if my mother had any other plans for me, or Millie, and then I'd head home to Bella. I was specifically told to leave her home today. That should have been a clue as to the type of party it was going to be. Usually my dog was welcome at backyard parties. Everyone loved a small dog, especially one who lapped up their attention like she did. But with this crowd, Bella wouldn't receive enough attention and she'd probably be too demanding.

Okay, so my little baby girl might, and I mean *might*, be a bit spoiled. But come on, I'm a thirty-one-year-old single man with no kids. I should have someone to love on, right?

Not that I'd blame Bella, but these people wouldn't want a loving dog sidling up to them, rubbing up against their expensive pant legs and leaving her hair. Or begging at the perfectly sandaled and manicured feet of a lady wearing a dress.

"Corbin, good to see you, man." Jake Anderson walked up with his date. He seemed to have a different woman every month. I wondered if he had subscribed to some sort of "Date of the Month" program. I couldn't remember him sticking with anyone past the last day of the month. I knew a new month had started when he showed up with someone new.

Jake and I had always been good friends. We'd played football together in high school and stayed in touch when we attended different colleges. Like so many of our friends, we ended up back in Southern California, and close to Corona, once we began our careers.

"Jake, glad you could make it. How was the drive through the canyon?" Like me, Jake had moved to Orange County for a job. But unlike me, he'd stayed there and only came back to town for special events, like today.

"Backed up as usual. Even the FastTrac lane took forever. But I guess it's to be expected now that everything is open again. With the great weather, who wants to stay indoors anymore?" Jake took the hand of the woman standing next to him. "Corbin, I'd like to introduce you to Sonya." He turned to his latest girlfriend. "Sonya, this is Corbin and my best friend."

The woman was pretty, but she also seemed aloof. When she first eyed me, I could have sworn she'd written me off. Probably because I wasn't dressed like everyone else. Then, when we were introduced, she seemed to take more interest in me. I noticed her brown eyes checking me out. Her auburn hair picked up the sunlight and glinted with hints of red and blond, which made me wonder if it was natural or if she had some of those different colors artistically added in just the right places to make it appear natural.

"Nice to meet you, Sonya. How did you meet Jake?" I tried to wrack my brain thinking if he'd told me or not, but I couldn't keep his dates straight, so a few years ago I stopped trying to remember anything about them. The only things I could remember were that they were all pretty. And most of them, like Sonya, were anywhere between five feet seven inches and five feet ten inches. The perfect height for Jake, who was over six feet tall.

Sonya turned smoldering eyes to my buddy. "We met at the beach last month."

Jake had eyes only for Sonya, so it must have been early in their month. But wait, if Jake had met her last month, and it was already the end of June... I shook my head and decided not to worry about it. If Jake dated this chick into next month, then I'd think more about her and where this might be going.

"The beach? Were you surfing without me?" Incredulity entered my voice. Jake never surfed without me.

My friend shook his head. "Nah, I was there with a group of buddies after work getting fish tacos when this vision of loveliness showed up." Jake took her hand and kissed it.

Which prompted me to take a closer look at the woman. She was pretty. Probably a step above the other women my friend dated, but she gave off an air of superiority. That wasn't something Jake usually went for. He was the happy-go-lucky type of guy who was friends with everyone. Sonya? She wouldn't approve of half of our friends. And if the looks she gave me earlier were any indication, she wouldn't approve of me.

Now I was feeling like a third wheel. The intensity between the two was more than I wanted to stick around for. "Say, have you seen Millie yet?"

That got Jake's attention. He blinked a few times and turned a huge grin my way. "Yeah, she's here with one of those Ivy League schmucks her mom's always trying to get her to go out with. I think he went to Stanford?" He shrugged.

"Harvard." Sonya smirked at me. It seemed she thought more highly of Millie's date than she did of me. She must not have seen the video of Millie yet. "But even that won't help her avoid the stigma associated with her fall from grace." She giggled at her own little joke, which really wasn't a joke.

This chick came into Millie's parents' house and had already started saying rude comments? Did she like that Millie had humiliated herself? Was she just another Melinda? Either way, this woman was trouble with a capital T.

I was going to have to have a long talk with Jake. But I'd wait until next month. For surely he'd get rid of her next week, right?

I raised a brow. "Really? Where is the happy couple now?" I turned my head, looking around, and found Millie on the opposite side of the backyard, as far from the pool as she could get while still being outside. It figured. She wasn't going to risk falling in again or ending up in an embarrassing situation. Who could blame her?

My first thought was how beautiful she was and my heart skipped a beat. This was the first time I'd seen her in I don't know how long, other than when she was covered in mud. And man, I wish I would have seen her before she entered that store. Maybe then we would have ended up on speaking terms and even attending this party together...as a date.

Then I realized she wasn't having a good time.

If the look on her face was any indication, she needed rescuing. To anyone else, she was happy and smiling. But I could see the strain in her smile. Her eyes were dull and lifeless, and she barely showed her teeth when she smiled. Normally if Millie was happy, her smile brightened her eyes and went from ear to ear. Her pearly whites were on display and one *felt* her joy.

I hadn't spent much time in her company since high school, but I knew her. Probably better than the Harvard dork at her side who looked like he had something stuck up his backside.

Slowly, I made my way toward her. One thing I had learned over the years was that when Millie was in a mood, you had to treat her like a skittish dog. The only way to approach her was slowly, and without expectation. If she thought for one second I was going to walk up to her, she'd completely shut down. Actually, she'd find an excuse to leave.

Around me, the backyard décor was a winter wonderland in summer. The little light displays had white-and-blue lights mixed throughout them. The snowman was large but tastefully done. It wasn't round; instead, it was flat and the lights had been twisted and turned throughout the metal rods that formed the snowman's hoops. There was even a black hat on top—flat, of course—but it had white light weaved through it.

The lights were all on, but not easy to see in the afternoon sunshine. In one corner sat an ice sculpture of what must have been a Christmas tree, but since the heat was melting the creation, it was difficult to tell. Thankfully it was on its own pedestal and there was an artful pan below it capturing the water as it melted off the ice block. This wasn't going to create a mud puddle.

Mrs. Milan had thought of everything. Or her decorator had. The tables around the backyard had red linen table cloths with varying flower displays on each. But the one thing in common were the red holly berries.

I chuckled, wondering if she had even picked out the white mistletoe that was so common in December. I looked for it, but I couldn't find any. Maybe because mistletoe was a winter plant?

I walked by a stand of red poinsettias in detailed pots, but when I touched one leaf, I realized they were fake. It made sense. Maybe if the florists had time, they could have ensured that all of our regular

Christmas flowers were in bloom this summer, but the fake ones were just as pretty.

With Millie in the corner of my eye, I continued to slowly meander through the backyard, checking out the various Christmas displays and talking to people I barely knew. If I could be sneaky in my approach, she might not even notice me until I was standing right next to her.

Hopefully after the plan her parents and mine had concocted, she'd stay here, even if she'd do all she could to avoid me.

Chapter 13

Millie

Why oh why did I agree to this? The guy standing next to me was a total and complete bore. I'd met snails more interesting than this guy. When my mother told me his name, I should have known. Who names their kid Tipton when their last name is Marks? I mean really, Tipton Marks? That was a recipe for disaster. Poor guy. Not like he could help it. With that name and his looks, he had to be a snoozefest.

The guy was handsome, too handsome if you asked me. He was tall, like really tall. He was taller than Corbin, probably six feet four or five inches tall. While Corbin had sultry green eyes, Tipton had blue eyes like the sea on a calm day. His blond hair looked like something out of *GQ* magazine. It was messy, but styled messy. Not truly a "Hey, I just out of bed and couldn't be bothered to do anything with my hair" kind of look. Nothing like what Corbin used to look like after he played football in the backyard with his friends...

Wait, what? Ugh, I really needed to get Corbin off my brain. Since seeing him at the mall during the *incident*, I couldn't stop thinking about him. Just last month I had actually fantasized that we would be friends again. But how could that happen when all he ever did was see me at my worst?

Speaking of which, Corbin was here. My mom had told me he couldn't make it. She said he had to work or something. Why did I agree to this again? I mean, come on. It was a Christmas pool party where no one, and I mean no one, was in their bathing suit, or looking anything like they were celebrating Christmas. Okay, so maybe Corbin was up for the whole Christmas in July theme, but other than my parents' Christmas decorations, it didn't look or feel like Christmas to me.

I had to do a double take when I realized Corbin was wearing a Christmas-themed, Hawaiian-print shirt. Was that Santa surfing? Oh boy. He was taking this a bit too far. Maybe he was working and had only come over for a few minutes? That would make sense for how he was dressed at the moment.

Figgy pudding, he'd caught me looking at him. I had to turn my head away when he grinned at me. Immediately, my palms began to sweat and my heart started pounding like the Little Drummer Boy when he played for Jesus' birth.

Where was the nearest exit? Oh, right. I couldn't leave. And I had better pay attention to what my date was saying.

"Did you see the match yesterday? Rafael Nadal isn't having a great year, is he?" It figured Tipton was into tennis. One of the sports I didn't know anything about.

Hold the horses! Was he talking to me, or to the other guy in our little circle?

Another Ivy League schmuck, Kingston Brown, was standing with us and I hoped against all hope that they were talking tennis to each other and didn't expect my input. When both men turned to look at me, I inwardly cringed. But on the outside, I frowned. "Yes, I'd have to agree with you, Tipton."

"Oh, I don't know. I think he's just getting warmed up." Kingston added his two cents.

Which only made me like him more. His disagreement got their attention off me and the two of them went on to talk stats and other tennis players. Some of the names I recognized, but that was all.

While they were distracted, I noticed Corbin edging even closer to us. Was it my imagination, or was he trying to stealthily get near me? Oh, please tell me he wasn't trying to come talk to me.

No, nope, not gonna allow that to happen. All I needed was for him to say something about the incident and get people talking about me in a way I didn't need. I was only with Tipton to keep that topic off me. People were much more interested in who I dated than what I'd done almost a week ago, weren't they?

I quickly finished my iced tea and motioned to Tipton that I wanted more, but of course he wasn't paying attention. While Corbin was busy talking to one of our other neighbors, I decided to sneak away to the refreshments table. Maybe I'd even get some food.

Although, I was trying very hard to keep from making any embarrassing mistakes today. So far, so good. If I could stay away from the pool, which now had a fence around it to keep clumsy people like me from falling in, then I might be alright. The next issue to tackle would be eating without making a mess.

I swear I was born without some gene that kept me from making the most embarrassing mistakes of my life whenever it mattered.

Oh, cake! I loved chocolate cake with strawberry filling and white frosting. I knew that was exactly what my mom had ordered from the caterers. There were also finger foods and a few tiny sandwiches with the crusts cut off. It was more like a giant tea party than a backyard barbecue.

Personally, I would have loved getting the grill going and throwing some dogs and burgers on the fire. That would have made for a much better party in my book. But my parents were a bit on the snooty side. They were nice and treated everyone with respect, but still, they tended to cater to those with a more delicate palate. These people wouldn't care for messy burgers or dripping hot dogs.

It was probably a good thing my mom had less messy food. With my luck, I'd end up dropping the cheeseburger down the front of my dress and making an even bigger fool of myself. And since the main focus now was to ensure people forgot about my uh, less-than-graceful exit from that horrid shop, I decided to stick with the finger foods.

Maybe there would be some cake left over after the party and I could eat it to my heart's content. But for now, I would eat like the bird I was supposed to be. Other than the clothes and lack of regular bathing, I could totally understand how the Regency era women felt. Okay, okay, so we have the right to vote and hold office now. Our clothes are much more comfortable and we won't be ostracized for wearing pants, but we *are* still expected to eat very little.

"Hey there. How goes it?" The unwelcome voice sent a chill down my spine and I cursed myself for not paying better attention to where Corbin was. For he obviously was trying to find me.

I gulped before turning around. "Corbin, how good to see you again." It wasn't. My cheeks flushed, and I decided I'd better be honest with myself. It was good to see him again. Drats, why did he still know how to make my heart go pitter-patter when he was near?

He motioned to his shirt. "Sorry, but I thought it was a Christmas party, not a socialite party."

I chuckled. I had thought the same until this morning, when my mother handed me the dress I was wearing. It was similar to the one in that store that shall forever be banned from my list of acceptable places to shop. The sleeveless bodice did show off my arms nicely, just like I thought. But the skirt wasn't as nice as the other one. This one was form-fitting instead of flouncy and limited my movements, but it did have spandex, so when I walked the flower-patterned skirt moved with my legs.

"Yeah, I thought the same until this morning. But really, this is Evelyn Milan we're talking about. She never does anything casual." I think I would have enjoyed it more if I could have been in capris and a tank top. I know I would have been cooler. Today must have been edging toward one hundred. What happened to our typical June gloom? If I wasn't mistaken, we'd seen the last of the nice, warm days and were headed to the dreadful, hot days.

"True, true." Corbin looked down at the food. "I take it the lunch is as fantastic as usual?"

"Yes, grab a plate and try for yourself. Mom used her normal caterers and I think you'll love the dessert." Or at least, I assumed he still enjoyed the chocolate strawberry cake like I did.

"Oooh, is that our favorite cake?" He pointed to the end of another table that housed the desserts, including a chocolate fountain. Which was something I would never in a million years go near during a party. Did I mention I was a klutz with the worst luck ever?

"Actually, yes, it is."

"And I take it you're going to wait until everyone is gone before even getting near the dessert table?" He still knew me too well.

I grimaced.

"Well, how about I dunk a few pieces of fruit in the chocolate fountain for you and we head over to some chairs to sit down and enjoy the feast?"

Corbin was being kind and cordial. What happened to the teenaged boy who would tease me mercilessly? Did he finally grow up?

"That sounds nice, thank you. But how about we just get a quick snack for now and walk and talk?" I still wasn't sure about eating. Because you know, I'm a klutz. And whatever can go wrong usually does go wrong for me.

And this new Corbin, well, I didn't want to take a chance and ruin this opportunity to talk to him in public. Besides, my current *date* was an absolute bore.

Corbin eyed me up and down and then looked to the table of food. When a sparkle entered his eyes, I began to get nervous. Was he going to play a prank on me? Was he still the same old Corbin who'd end up making things worse for me? I prayed he wouldn't do anything to ruin my already shredded reputation.

"I see what you're doing." He rubbed his chin. "Millie, I'll help you. If you're hungry, I can get you a plate. We may not have been the best of buds lately, but I do still know you, Millicent Milan."

"Ugh, using my full name?" I hated my full name. Millicent—really? Who named their kid that in this day and age? It may have been popular a hundred years ago, but this was the twenty-first century, not the nineteen-hundreds. Okay, I know that didn't make much sense seeing as how I was born at the very end of the nineteen-hundreds, but really, my parents should have known it was a very outdated name.

Corbin chuckled. Not loudly, but enough to catch the attention of the couple near us. He waved. "Hello, Mr. and Mrs. Benson. Nice to see you again."

The Bensons weren't our neighbors, but they were a couple my parents had been socializing with for years. I smiled and waved.

After the niceties were exchanged, they moved along. I could see Mrs. Benson eyeing me warily. She probably wanted to get as far away from me as she could. Guilt by association? Or was she afraid I'd pull her down in the mud with me? Or push her into the pool? She was there that night of the pool incident, and she was probably remembering it.

My parents did install that fancy fence right after that event, to make sure no one else fell in. Or at least, that's what they said. But I always knew it was in case I fell in again. They ended up baby-proofing the house thanks to my *accidents*. I wouldn't call them accidents, but I did know I had the worst luck ever.

So really, who could blame anyone for wanting to get as far away from me as possible? The fact that Corbin was still near me, and wanted to continue to be so, well, that was shocking.

"Alright, so what would you like to eat, *Millie*?" He stressed my nickname, and all was forgiven.

As usual, I had eaten before the party. Since I was known to have...well...let's just call them accidents, I always ate before parties. Especially the backyard variety. I did alright at sit-down dinners. My issues usually stemmed from the standing-around-and-eating sort of parties. It seemed I couldn't even chew gum and walk at the same time.

"How about two of the salmon pâté sandwiches?" Those were my favorites. And if I focused on eating one at a time, I should be alright. Key word—*should*.

The conversation with Corbin was wonderful. He told me all about his job and moving to Orange County, then back home to Corona. I was starting to feel my old friend was back. I didn't have any romantic feelings for him, not like when we were kids.

It was only a very strong attraction. Because, come on, Corbin was still one of the hottest guys I'd ever seen. But it was just skin deep, right?

However, the friendly vibes I was getting from him soothed me and helped me to relax. It was like the parties we attended together growing up. He always got me food to help keep me from spilling or making a scene, and we talked. Really talked.

When we found ourselves in the back corner of the yard with no one in hearing distance, he surprised me. "Millie, I am so sorry for everything. I wish we could get back these past fourteen years. Can you ever forgive me?"

I felt the prick of tears coming on, my nose was starting to burn, and if he was any sweeter, I'd have a toothache. "Corbin, I've missed you." And I had. We were best friends. He was all over my earliest memories. It was almost as though we were siblings when we were really little. Everyone commented on how much time we spent together as little kids. Then, when we hit puberty, speculation began about us getting together.

Corbin never saw me as anything other than his friend and adopted sister. I even heard him say that once. And I never thought of him as anything more than... Who was I kidding? I was in love with the boy not long after puberty hit. But I didn't realize it until junior year of high school.

I had high hopes for that night, and that dress. But it was Melinda who showed me up and caught his attention. I thought for sure he would have asked her out after that night. I mean, come on, she was H.O.T. hot. A bit on the slutty side, but still one of the most beautiful girls in high school. I was really surprised it took several months before she was able to get him to go out with her.

And if the rumors could be believed, a sure thing. One date with her and the boys would hit a home run. Back then, the expected wait time was at least five dates, but not with Melinda. She was a one-date sorta girl, but only if you got her to say yes to a date.

I saw one of her friends out of the corner of my eye and prayed she wouldn't show. From what I'd heard, she was still the same slutty Melinda as she'd been as a teenager. In fact, the current rumor was that her husband was suing her for divorce and full custody of their two kids. Apparently she was a rotten mother. Not surprising when I thought about her mother. The apple really didn't fall from the tree in that family.

"I've missed you, too, Millie." Corbin licked his lips. "Do you think we can start over? Be friends again?"

Chapter 14

Millie

Starting over didn't seem right. We had so much history. How could one start over with our history? "I don't know."

Corbin's head hung and he tried again. "Millie, can you at least forgive me?"

That I could do. "Yes, I forgave you a long time ago."

He tilted his head and looked into my eyes. "Really? Then why did you never reach out to me?"

Heat suffused my cheeks and I looked down. "Because I was embarrassed."

Corbin had the ability to chew gum and walk at the same time—he always had. So he put the plate and napkins in one hand and with his other he took one of mine. "Millie, there's no need to be embarrassed. You're my best friend. Always have been, and always will be. I'm here to stand by you."

So my parents and his had orchestrated this reunion? He was called on to help me? I pulled my hand away. "Corbin, I'm sorry you feel the need to rescue me yet again, but it's not needed."

"Millie, that's not what today is about."

I started to walk away, and he dropped the plates and took both of my hands in his.

"Listen to me. I've wanted us to make up ever since that night I saw you in that sexy black dress. I know I screwed up, big time. And I've regretted my actions ever since that night. But can we please get past it? I want us to be friends again." The earnest expression on his face hit my heart.

"Corbin, wait. What? You remember my dress?" Of all the things I could have asked, I had no idea why that question was what came out.

He grinned. "Yes, it's been etched on my brain for these fourteen years. I'll never forget how sexy you looked that night. And I'm so sorry for destroying your dress. But I was worried it would weigh you down in the pool. I had to make sure you could get out."

"But, I thought..." Was he looking at me that night? With Melinda basically naked, how could anyone look anywhere but at her? "Wasn't it Melinda who caught your attention? Isn't that why you threw the ball at me?"

The sigh that escaped Corbin spoke volumes. He was exasperated with me, and I knew it. He probably thought I looked terrible that night and his way of saving me was to push me into the pool with his football. Surely he wasn't attracted to me. No man would throw a football at a woman he was attracted to, would he?

"You thought Melinda caught my eye? But why would I throw the ball at you if that was the case?" He quirked a brow and looked confused.

"Because you thought I looked horrible?" That had to be it. Otherwise, no. I wasn't going there.

Corbin's light chuckle sent tendrils of delight up and down my spine. "Millie, I threw the ball exactly where I was looking. It was a total mistake. I had the ball and was about to throw it to Jake when you walked into my line of sight. I stopped and turned to face you and was absolutely entranced by your beauty."

"Then why did you throw the ball at me?" He had to be mistaken—or lying to protect my ego. Right?

"Silly Millie. A football player always throws the ball where they're looking. When I saw you and froze, Jake screamed at me to throw the ball. So I did. Only I didn't turn back to him first. I was out of my mind. I couldn't believe how beautiful you were. And what a woman you'd become. One second you were this punk kid I grew up with and my best friend. I'd never really noticed you were a girl. In that moment, everything changed." The tenderness in Corbin's eyes melted my frozen heart.

I was about to cry when he pulled me in for a hug. We were making up? After all this time, we were really and truly making up? I had forgiven him, but did I trust him? I should. That much I knew. But all of my memories were a jumble.

And my emotions...

Oh drummer boy, my emotions. His big, strong arms around me felt safe, warm, and something else. My heart pitter-pattered like in those romance books and I knew I was falling hard...again. I couldn't do this. I pulled back out of his arms and a nervous chuckle escaped my lips. "Well, now that we have that cleared up, how about some dessert?"

If we didn't get back to the party, I was going to burst with crazy emotions. All of my unrequited feelings were surging forth. I thought

I had smothered them so well that they'd never surface again. Boy was I wrong.

"Millie, are you alright?" Corbin took one of my hands.

I nodded. I wasn't alright, but I couldn't admit that. Instead, I needed to put my game face on. Be the society woman my mother had taught me to be. She'd instilled in me from a young age the necessary wisdom of not letting them see your emotions. It wasn't a lesson I took to very well, but I did have the knowledge, and now was the time to put it to good use.

I thought of spreadsheets and tennis—two of the most boring things in the world. That ought to erase any emotions from my face. Then I straightened my shoulders and blinked a few times. "Corbin, how about we head back into the party? I don't want anyone to worry about us."

Not that I cared about my date, but it was a valid excuse. And besides, if we stood here talking or hugging any longer, I'd totally break out in tears. And that wouldn't do my reputation any good.

Confusion covered Corbin's face and I knew he would want an explanation, but he too was raised to keep emotions off his face in public. We had been back here alone for long enough. And after that hug, people would be watching us. Everyone knew that our friendship had died in high school.

"Alright, let's go get something to drink. I'm parched. The heat isn't helping at all." Corbin put his elbow out for me and I took it.

With my penchant for tripping over my own feet, I thought this was a good idea. But touching him sent a thrill through my entire being.

On the one hand, I was beyond happy that we had finally made up. And that I had learned what really went on that night. But on the other, I was horrified to realize that I still had feelings for Corbin.

While he may have finally noticed I was a woman when we were seventeen, there was no way on candy cane lane he would have any sort of attraction for me. Friendship? That I could see. But attraction now? No way. I was a novelty, like a reindeer with a red nose. Plus, his mom had probably roped him into helping me.

Maybe this whole afternoon was nothing more than him trying to help an old friend get out of a jam. And tomorrow he'd forget all about me again. That would give me time to get my emotions under control and then I'd be able to move forward. I could talk to him and be in his company without a problem. Yes, that was it. That was all this was about—duty.

Neither of us spoke to each other. There really wasn't a chance. As we walked to the dessert table, people looked at us and stopped us. Some asked Corbin questions, while others asked me questions. But everyone wanted to know if we were friends again. It seemed all of the attention was back on me.

Weren't we supposed to keep the attention *away* from me?

My face hurt trying to keep a smile plastered on as we moved slower than an iceberg toward the dessert table. Although, with this heat, moving any faster would have produced sweat. The last thing I needed was a sweaty brow messing up my makeup and bangs.

After what felt like an hour, but was probably more like fifteen minutes, we finally made it to the table full of sugary concoctions. And the bowl of lemonade. I went toward the liquid gold and Corbin followed.

"Here, let me." He took the ladle and poured us each a small glass.

I knew better than to down the drink, so I took slow, small sips, all the while praying I wouldn't have a hole in my lips. So far, I hadn't made a mess of anything. But I had made a cake of myself with the hug and alone time that everyone seemed to have noticed.

People all around whispered and pointed. I sighed. It was no use; I'd never get out of the gossip. Maybe I should move to a deserted island and spend the rest of my days alone? No one would be able to see me doing anything embarrassing and gossip about me. The only problem with that was I'd miss my parents. And Bella.

Corbin's dog was the cutest thing ever. I had even been thinking about getting one of my own. I loved how she knew exactly when I needed a little bit of loving attention and when I needed to play. I wished she was here with us now. She'd pull everyone's attention away from me and onto her.

But she wasn't here.

I was going to have to be a big girl and ignore the stares and finger-pointing. Gah, my mother would kill me if I pointed at people like they were. Didn't any of them have a prim and proper upbringing like I did? Probably not.

Not that it really helped me, anyways.

"What would you like?" Corbin waved over the table and my mouth watered as I took in the variety of sugary goodness.

With all eyes on me, I knew I couldn't do the chocolate fountain, or even the cake. I needed something small I could nibble on without too much mess. "How about a chocolate crisp cookie?"

Corbin nodded and picked up a cookie and a napkin. "Your treat, my lady." He bowed in front of me with his hand out, holding the treat for me to take.

I couldn't resist a little curtsy in response and a light giggle. "Thank you, Corbin."

All went well, which shocked me. I mean really shocked me. I didn't even get a single crumb down the front of my dress. God was smiling down on me. I should have gone with that and been happy, but no. I had to go and press my luck.

"Do you think we could try something from the chocolate fountain?" I licked my lips as I took in the display of fruits and breads just waiting to be dipped.

"I thought you'd never ask." Like me, Corbin had always loved the chocolate fountain.

As kids, he would get a plate full of fruit and pound cake, then dip them all with the cute little skewers and bring the plate to me. We'd go find a seat off to the side and eat until we were stuffed. Even back then I knew better than to get near something so dangerous as a chocolate fountain. When I was only seven, I accidentally tipped the table while I was trying to dip a strawberry. You can guess what happened.

After that, I was never allowed within five feet of the fountain, or the dessert table.

I wasn't about to get close to the desserts, just in case, but I did stand six feet away and watched as he dipped not only the various fruits into the chocolate fountain, but also pound cake and a few donut holes. Then he went and picked up two pieces of cake.

If I wasn't careful, I'd gain ten pounds and pop the buttons on the back of my dress. This was a bad idea; I never had good ideas when I was around society people.

With my plate in one hand, I began chewing on the nails of my other hand—a bad habit I thought my mother had trained out of me before I even went to middle school. But maybe not? This day was starting to really unnerve me. So far, nothing had gone wrong.

Could it be that I'd get through this event with Corbin without a dramatic event?

I smiled when Corbin motioned his head for me to follow him. He led us to a line of chairs just outside the clear fence surrounding our pool. The fence was low, since we didn't have any kids, but it did help to keep people from being pushed into the cold water. A feeling of excitement overcame me as I realized he and I were having a nice time together. He wasn't teasing me, pulling my pigtails, or pushing me into the water.

Okay, so I didn't have pigtails for him to pull, and with the waist-high clear plexiglass fence, it was a little difficult for him to push me in. And we hadn't really talked long enough for him to have a chance to tease me, but hey, it was still going well.

Corbin took the end seat, and I took the seat between him and Mrs. Green. She was another neighbor from down the street. While she was a bit loud, and part of the gossip chain, she was a bit hard of hearing if she didn't have her hearing aids in. And she never wore them to parties; she said it gave her a headache to hear all of that noise.

I never knew her to be blind before, but she must be.

When I sat down, I not only felt the moosh, but I heard the splat as well as the laughs from those around me.

Mrs. Green turned to me. "Oh, dear. I'm so sorry. I didn't hear you approaching." She felt around her head. "Nor did I see you." She proceeded to put her glasses on. "Oh, Millie. I'm so sorry. I didn't mean to put my cake on your seat."

I'd looked, honestly I had, before turning around to take the seat next to Corbin. The old coot must have put the plate under my backside as I was going down. There was no way I could have known she was going to put her uneaten cake down. She should have looked where she was setting her plate. For all she knew, there may have already been plates of food sitting next to her. Or someone sitting there.

In my brand-new dress, I had sat down on the cake I was afraid to eat because I might spill it on myself and make a scene. Instead, Mrs. Green put her cake underneath me as I was taking the seat and did the deed for me.

Chapter 15

C orbin

"Millie. I'm so sorry." I should have seen it coming. We were finally talking and not arguing. She wasn't being hauled off to the security office dripping wet with mud or pool water. She had made it through at least two hours of an important party without making a cake of it—pun totally intended—only to have me show up and ruin everything.

How in the world was I supposed to help her if I couldn't even check her seat before she sat down? And that dress! Oh drummer boy was that dress hot. Now it was ruined. It showed off her shapely legs so well. And her other assets? Man oh man would most of the cheerleaders from high school be jealous of her today. Well, before Mrs. Green went and ruined everything for Millie.

Millie was so beautiful, even more so than when we were kids. When she smiled at me, my whole world brightened like a sunny day after a week straight of rain and black clouds.

I was walking on air, until we sat down and the walls came crumbling.

Everyone in the back backyard was looking at us. Several were laughing. And of course, one of Melinda's besties was here and she was taking pictures on her phone. If I knew Suzy, she was already posting on social media and tagging Melinda.

This was the exact opposite of what we needed for today. This party was supposed to be Millie's opportunity to shine and have everyone forget what a klutz she was. Now she'd forever be remembered as the person with the most issues, and one who couldn't even sit down without causing a scene.

"That's it. I'm done," Millie whispered, and tilted her head down to avoid the stares. She left me standing there gaping at her backside.

The moment my mind began working again, I ran to follow her. As we passed one of the food tables, I picked up a stack of paper napkins and tried to brush the strawberries and icing off her backside.

The moment I touched her, I realize what I'd done. The laughs stopped and the intake of breaths was even louder than the whispered comments. I had made one of the biggest mistakes a man could make: I'd touched the bottom of a woman who wasn't my wife or girlfriend. I didn't do it in a leering way; I was only trying to help clean up the mess. But no one would retell the story that way. People would leave off the fact that there was cake all over her backside and just tell other that I was grabbing her butt as she ran from me.

Hmm, that might not be too bad. I wouldn't look good, but the women would at least feel sorry for Millie instead of laughing at her. But, would that be any better?

Probably not.

I'd keep my hands to myself, but I would be close behind her to help keep as many prying eyes, and lenses, away from her cake-covered behind as I could.

I could only imagine some of the online comments that would be coming from the pics Suzy shared. "Millie, what can I do to help?"

"Just leave me alone. I knew this was a bad idea. I told my parents, and yours, that I shouldn't be allowed out in public right now." Millie sighed and turned around when she arrived at the bottom of the stairs. "Look, I don't blame you for this. And really, I can't blame Mrs. Green. She's an old lady with hearing and vision impairments."

She threw her hands in the air. "It's just my bad luck. If you're smart, you'll stay clear of me. I'm a bomb waiting to go off when anyone from society gets near me." Without waiting for a reply, she turned and fled upstairs.

I could have followed; it wasn't like I didn't know where her childhood room was located. But I wouldn't. She obviously needed to change and clean up. The best course of action was to give her space and time. In a few days, I'd stop by her house for a visit and to check in on her.

Which was exactly what I did two days later.

Bella and I both stood waiting patiently at Millie's front door. So much had happened in the past two days, and none of it had anything to do with Millie. The entire way there I'd asked Bella what she thought. But of course, my little black-and-white Boston Terrier could only tilt her head and look at me as though I was crazy.

Which I probably was.

"Come on, Millie. I have some really great news." When no one answered, I decided to let her know I knew she was home. Her car was in the driveway, and right now there was no way she'd be out and about with anyone else.

A sound came from the other side of the door and I assumed she was looking through her peephole. When the door didn't open, I leaned down and picked up Bella. I knew without a shadow of a doubt that my dog's perfectly cute button nose held up to the peephole would break down any barriers to entry.

When the lock clicked, I knew bringing Bella was the right move.

"Bella." A sweet, small smile spread across Millie's face as she leaned down and kissed the top of my dog's head.

"Woof." Bella licked Millie's face and jumped on her. And Millie took it all in stride.

I smiled down on my two favorite girls. My girls? As in both were mine? Where in the world did that thought come from? Sure, Bella was mine. But Millie? At one time I would have thought she was mine, but not in a romantic way. She was *my* best friend for half my life. Until I noticed she was no longer the little girl with pigtails I used to yank on.

And now? Whoa, now she was a beautiful woman who sent my heart pounding. All of a sudden, I didn't know what I was doing. Sweat pooled on my forehead and a few drops went down my back. I tried to tell myself it was just the heat. Outside was over one hundred degrees today, so that must have been it.

"Corbin? Corbin, did you hear me?" Millie's forehead was bunched up and she stared at me funny.

I looked down to see Bella giving me the same exact look.

Then I realized that Millie had been asking me something. I licked my lips. "I'm sorry? What was that?"

The vision in a patriotic red, white, and blue tie-dye shirt and denim shorts waved me to enter her house. "I said, why don't you come in?" She arched a brow.

A quick chuckle escaped my lips as I walked past her into a house I'd never been inside before. Just from the entryway I could tell she had great taste. Her mother's taste would be described as exquisite, but Millie's would be more comfortable and welcoming.

"Please, take your shoes off and join me for iced tea. You must be thirsty after standing outside in that heat."

I did as she bid and noticed that the floor looked like some sort of fancy distressed wood, but it felt more like a tile floor. After taking a closer look, I noticed it was long planks of porcelain tiles designed to look like distressed wood, but were in fact a matte tile. Zero shine or gloss here. Grout separated the pieces that were about eight by thirty-six inches.

I had recently seen something like this in my local home improvement store, but I had yet to see anyone using it in their home. I liked it. It was great for the summer as the floor felt cool to my feet, even though it was so hot outside.

"I like your tile. It's nice and cool. But what about during the winter? We don't get much in the way of freezing temps, but it does get cold here."

Her smile warmed my heart. "I have throw rugs I put out when it's cold. And of course I wear slippers during the winter." She shrugged. "You like this design?"

I nodded.

Bella noticed we were looking at the floor and she sniffed it before letting loose a quiet chuff. It seemed my dog liked it too.

Maybe I'd have to look into something like this for my condo. It would be much easier to clean up after a messy dog with something like this instead of carpet. Although, Bella was housetrained so she only made a mess in the pantry, where her water was kept.

"You're such a pretty girl. Yes you are." Millie scratched behind Bella's ears, and my dog's back leg began to shake.

"How do you know my dog so well?"

"When you leave her with your parents, I spend quite a bit of time with her. In fact, two months ago when you were gone for a week, Bella came to visit me for a few days. She's the perfect house guest."

When Millie stood up, Bella barked and ran to the living room.

My dog knew exactly where to go, so I followed. In the corner of the living room, next to the gas fireplace, was a dog bed and a few toys for Bella. She went right over and picked up a squeaky pig and then brought it to Millie. I'd never seen Bella share her toys with anyone else before.

I wasn't sure if I should be happy or jealous.

Once we were both seated with iced teas in hand, Millie turned to me and arched a brow. "What can I do for you today, Corbin?"

I would have thought she'd be happy to see me. Instead, she was happy to see my dog. "I came by to check in on you. After the party the other day, I wasn't sure how you'd be doing."

"I'm fine. I've stayed off social media and I even took a few days off from work." She took a long sip of her tea.

I could tell she wasn't fine. If she took time off work just because of all this, then she was hiding. And that wasn't a good thing to do. A sudden ache passed through my chest and I wondered if I'd pulled a muscle, or if it was the beginnings of a heart attack. Pain went down my left arm and I felt very uncomfortable.

"Uh, what have you been doing all day?" The easy camaraderie we'd begun to share right before she sat in cake was gone. Now, a feeling of unease permeated the room.

"Cleaning. And watching movies." Millie turned away from me and looked to Bella, who sat at her feet.

"Christmas movies?" When we were kids, she loved to watch Christmas movies. She began watching them on Black Friday after she was done shopping with our moms, and then continued non-stop all the way through New Year's. I used to watch the comedies with her. *Home Alone* was one of our all-time favorites.

She shook her head. "No. Absolutely not." Millie pursed her lips. "I'm so over Christmas right now. I'm not even sure if I'll be in the mood for it come December."

Right, the Christmas Crazy fiasco. I should have known.

"You do know that Christmas is more than just presents, right? It's really about the birth of our Lord and Savior." If I could get her to remember the reason for the season, maybe she could relax and enjoy it.

"Tell that to the rest of the world. It's become so commercialized, I doubt kids today even know the real reason." The disgust in her voice was strong. Not that I could blame her. She wasn't wrong.

"Care to watch *The Little Drummer Boy*?" We used to watch the little Claymation show that came with the set of movies titled: *Santa Claus is Coming to Town*, *Frosty the Snowman*, and *Rudolph the Red-Nosed Reindeer*. We would devote a whole night to those shows. I think my parents used to watch them when they were kids, but I always love them. Classic Christmas movies never went out of style.

"No, thanks. I think I'm just going to pass this year. It's not a bad idea to skip Christmas once in a while, you know?" She grinned, but it was only a half-hearted attempt.

"We skipped Christmas this past December, along with the rest of the world. Which is why Christmas in July is so popular this year. Come on, aren't you even watching those sappy Christmas romances on the Hallmark channel?" I didn't care for the Hallmark channel, but

I knew from my mom that the Milan ladies enjoyed watching those movies, as did my own mother.

"Nope, not doing the Hallmark movie marathons this year with our moms. I already told them they were on their own." Millie pursed her lips. "I was actually thinking I might start volunteering at the homeless shelter again, if they have need. Or I could take a quick trip to the orphanage in Africa. I haven't been there since the world opened back up, and I think it's time I went. I miss those kids."

While I hadn't been to the Ugandan Home for Children, the orphanage that the Milans supported, I had seen so many pictures and videos of the place. I was supposed to go after graduation with Millie for a month, but, well...yeah. "When do you think you'll go?"

"I think July twentieth through the thirtieth might be a good time. Not a lot of churches or other organizations will want to be away from home at that time, and I think I might be able to do some good. Plus, I really miss them. FaceTime just isn't good enough, you know?" Her lips tweaked up on one side, almost like a smile.

Maybe it would be good for her to go. And maybe I could join her? "What would you think about delaying a few days and having a few tagalongs?" I knew her parents would go, as would mine, if given the chance. But they had so many events planned for Christmas in July that she'd need to work around their plans.

Millie tilted her head and stared at me. "You said before I opened the door that you had some news? What was it?"

Alright, she was going to ignore my request to join her on her mission trip. I'd let her drop it, for now. Maybe my news would help her. "I think you're forgotten by now."

When Millie was confused, she'd get this look in her eyes and the skin between her eyebrows would wrinkle. It was the cutest look ever.

Even better than when Bella tilted her head and gave me her knowing look. That was the look on Millie's face at that very moment.

Chapter 16

Millie

After Corbin and Bella left, I sat on my sofa wondering about everything Corbin had said. Could it be that I was in the clear? Would everyone forget about all of my klutzy moves lately?

If so, poor Melinda. I mean, she kinda deserved it. But that wasn't very nice of me to think. Our actions have consequences. Sometimes I wondered why I had so many issues when I wasn't a bad person. I didn't mess with married men—I was even waiting until I got married before I shared a bed with a man.

However, I wasn't perfect. So, could it be that I'd done a few things that had consequences? Like the kind that put me face-first in a mud bath while news cameras were recording? Could be. Or, it could be the enemy attacking me for the good things I did. Or, it could be just because there was evil in this world.

Whatever the reason, I couldn't judge Melinda for what she'd done. I could, however, pray for her and her family.

If she had fallen face-first into a vat of mud, I probably would have laughed at her and even liked and forwarded the social media posts. But this? No. It wasn't funny. What she'd done was the sort of thing that ruined families and careers.

While I was grateful that the attention was off me, I wasn't happy about why.

Getting caught in a cheesy hotel with one of our city council members, who was supposedly happily married, was a rotten thing. It was the sort of thing that would get him kicked off the council, even though he did a lot of good for our city. And it would give her soon-to-be ex more grounds for getting full custody of their kids.

Melinda was already in the middle of a tough divorce battle. This was only going to make things worse. And not only just for her, but for her kids as well as her husband.

At that very moment, a heavy heart brought me to my knees. I prayed for Melinda to get right with God, but more importantly, I prayed for her kids. I also prayed for the council member, Ron Jones, and his wife.

While I disagreed with divorce, I also knew there were valid reasons for one. Sleeping with another woman were grounds for Cindy Jones to seek a divorce from her husband of over thirty years. Thankfully, their kids were all grown.

Even though Ron had cheated on Cindy, I prayed that they could get counseling and work through these issues. I even prayed that Melinda and her husband could resolve their issues and stay together. To do that, Melinda would have to stop cheating on her husband and actually care for her kids.

Just as I was saying "Amen," my phone rang. "Hi, Mom. What's up?"

"Dear, did Corbin talk to you?"

I rolled my eyes. Of course she'd know about that already. "Yes, he did. Did you send him here?"

"Anna just told me Corbin was heading to your house earlier. Have you two patched things up?" A hopeful tone entered my mother's voice, causing me to wonder what was going on.

"Yes, we did. Why?" I sat down on the couch, knowing I wasn't going to be happy.

"The club is having their annual Fourth of July picnic next weekend. I was thinking that would be a wonderful time for you to make another appearance, now that the gossip is off of you." My mother's chipper voice caused a pang of regret to slice through my veins.

"Mother, just because the gossipmongers are focused on someone else doesn't mean I should be out and about. Besides, I don't want to contribute anything to poor Melinda's situation. It isn't just her who was hurt by this." What gossipers forgot about were the innocents in these situations. Melinda and Ron might be experiencing the just rewards of their actions, but their families didn't deserve the negative attention on them. No one actually deserved to be the center of malicious gossip. But it was one of the effects of sin. And sin they did.

However, it wasn't up to me to judge them, either. Nor was it right for the community to do so. Their pastors should speak with them, and they needed to get right with God, if they were believers. But all this finger-pointing and spreading rumors wasn't going to help anyone, especially Melinda's kids.

"Honey, I'm not saying we should participate in this...well...torrid affair. What I'm saying is that you need to be out and about. Don't say anything about Ron and Melinda. Ignore that situation. But if you're at the party, people will see you in a good light. Especially if you attend with Tipton. Everyone liked him. He's been quite the talk lately."

"Ugh, Mother. I'm not interested in Tipton. Sure, he's nice, but he's so boring. Total snoozefest. If he's my only choice, I'll stay home, thank you very much." Besides, staying home would be much preferable to subjecting myself to those people. People who turned on you the very second they smelled blood. They were worse than sharks.

At least you knew a shark was a predator and would always attack. This country club set would be sweet to your face, and then the moment anything came up, they'd attack you behind your back. All the while continuing to smile at you.

People were so exhausting. Why couldn't they be nice? I mean, really, how difficult was it to be nice to someone instead of attack? I always found that caring for people was truly the easier way. It's so much work to gossip and stab people in the back.

"Hm, well. If you don't want to go with Tipton, how about Jackson? He seemed interested in you at my party. And he's even asked about you."

Would my mother ever stop matchmaking?

I sighed. "Mom, Jackson's on the rebound. He's not a good date."

"But you would look so nice on his arm. Why not give him a chance? You've known him a long time. And his family is highly respected. There's not even a hint of scandal there."

How could I tell her that Jackson was a scandal just waiting to happen without being vulgar? "Ah, Mom. Jackson's not in the right frame of mind for dating someone like me."

"And what's that supposed to mean?" Her high-pitched reply informed me she was getting tired of my beating around the bush.

Alright, even though my mother couldn't see me, I squared my shoulders and stood tall in front of my fireplace. With no fire in the hearth, it wasn't quite as dramatic a scene, but then again, I'd had enough drama in my life lately. "Mom, there's something you should know about Jackson."

"Millie, he's a nice boy. Just the sort that would do your reputation justice."

"No, Mom. He's not. He's on the prowl."

I heard a throat clear on the other end of the line. "And just what is that supposed to mean?"

"It means, mother of mine, that Jackson Devencourt is only looking to get laid." There, I'd said it plain as day. There'd be no way she could try pushing him on me again after this.

My mother spluttered and coughed. "Language, Millie. Language. A lady never speaks about a man in that fashion." She sighed. My mother, the picture of decorum, actually sighed so hard I could hear it over the phone. "What makes you think this?"

I could picture her sitting at the table with her head in her hands. She wasn't exactly the sort to take part in gossip, and I didn't want to share gossip, either. Was it gossip if it was something that happened to me?

"Mom, at your party he came on to me in such a way that it left nothing to my imagination." The silence between us told me all I needed to know. "Now, I think I should stay home. Maybe staying out of the public eye a little bit longer would be good for me, and you."

My actions had never negatively impacted my parents' social standing. It wasn't as though I'd slept with a married man or robbed a store. I was a klutz, plain and simple. But as the daughter of a wealthy family with connections, that was almost a sin. It was definitely something worthy of gossip and finger-pointing.

And given the way my mother and Mrs. Deeks responded after the Christmas Crazy incident, I'm betting my parents received looks of pity. That was something a society woman just could not tolerate.

"Okay," she said, "then Corbin."

"What? What do you mean, Corbin?" Had I missed something? Maybe instead of speaking her thoughts out loud she had been musing to herself, and that last bit came out unintentionally?

"Dear, you need to attend this event with Corbin. Especially now that you two are friends again. It's perfect. People will see you and Corbin together, and if they want to talk about you it will only be about how nice it is to see the two of you being friends again. Or, if we're lucky, they'll talk about what a great couple you two make."

"Really, Mom? You *want* people talking about me?" I would be much happier being a turtle and hiding in my shell, where no one could see me for the next hundred years. Being in the public eye, even if it was only the Corona society eye, was nothing I ever enjoyed. Ever.

"Sweetheart, trust me. This is for your own good. When people talk kindly about you, it's a good thing. This will only serve to heighten your image."

"But, what about Corbin? Maybe he already has a date?" I hadn't seen him with another woman, or even heard anything about him dating. But that didn't mean he wanted to take me to this picnic. We'd only just patched things up. It was all so new and fragile.

"Don't worry. He'll be excited to take you as his date."

"Excited? Really, Mom?" I deadpanned through the phone. Somehow I knew that without being able to show the droll look on my face, it just wasn't the same over the phone as in person.

"Yes, I'll take care of everything. Don't worry. And be sure to get a new dress. Something in red would be nice with your complexion."

"Mom, if it's a picnic, why am I going to wear a dress?"

"Because, sweetie, this is the country club, not the country." She giggled at her own lame joke.

I didn't think I'd ever understand my mother's humor. But if all the women attending this shindig wore dresses, then I'd have to as well.

The next day when my phone rang, I cringed. It was either my mother telling me again what I needed to wear and who I needed to be seen with, or it was my boss telling me I was fired. I hadn't been into the office in quite a while.

I did, however, get a lot of work done. Who knew I could work so hard when not surrounded by cubicle mates who chatted all the time?

When I checked my caller ID, I cringed. "Hello, Mr. Baker."

It was my boss. Usually he sent me emails when he needed something. Phone calls weren't exactly something I received too often, even when the entire world was locked down and we'd worked from home for months straight.

"Miss Milan, good afternoon. I was wondering when you'd grace us with your presence again?" He didn't sound too happy.

While we did have the ability to work from home now, it wasn't supposed to be full-time. "Mr. Baker, sorry about that. I've been working hard on the Meeker account. I don't know if you've seen it, but I actually turned in the mock-ups three days early, and I was working on the next part of the assignment."

My hope was that if he saw how busy I'd been, and how good my work was, he'd be fine with me working from home.

"I did see it, and I liked what you did. But part of working in the office is interacting with your team. While you've been working away, they haven't been doing as well. I think it would be a good idea if you began coming in again. Since you're ahead on your work, you could help your teammates with their assignments. And maybe even show them how to be as hardworking as you."

Ah, that was it. He'd probably caught them at the water cooler too many times, chatting about everything under the sun. It was tough being back in the office again. Since everyone had been in lockdown for so long, it was nice to have company again. It was energizing to be in the presence of other people. Some people did well all alone, while others thrived on the energy of crowds.

Me? I was somewhere in the middle. I loved to be around people, but I could also recharge my inner reserves by being alone. Lately, however, I was hiding. And that wasn't good, either.

"Yes, sir. I'll be in the office first thing tomorrow morning." At least there I could get away with wearing slacks instead of a dress. It wasn't that I hated dresses, but every day? No thank you. I hated wearing nylons, and those were needed when wearing heels. I knew a lot of women didn't wear nylons anymore, but I felt it was better to hold in my not-so-slim stomach if I was going to wear a dress.

The dress pants that I wore all had a tummy tucking sheen inside. I wasn't exactly skinny, or even fashionably endowed. I liked food. Especially desserts. Put a chocolate éclair in front of me and I'd eat the entire thing.

My cubemate, Michael, always brought in eclairs on Fridays. His wife managed a bakery, and she made the absolute best pastries. Great, now I had dessert on the mind. And I'd be eating an éclair this Friday, I knew it.

Chapter 17

Corbin

When my mother first suggested I take Millie to the Fourth of July party at the club, I was hesitant. But then I thought about it and realized it was a genius idea. I'd be there with Millie the entire time, and I could look after her. Plus, we'd get to spend time getting to know one another again.

The only problem? I had feelings for the woman. Figgy pudding, but she was gorgeous. And the fact that she didn't even realize how beautiful she was made her even prettier. Even Jake had commented on how well Millie had grown up.

Speaking of Jake, I looked at my caller ID and smiled. "Jake, buddy. How goes it?"

The sound of an injured animal squeaked through the line. "She dumped me. How could she do that?"

"What? Who dumped you?" Since I wasn't sure who he was dating at the moment, I needed to know.

"Sonya, the love of my life," Jake bellowed.

"Uh, Jake, buddy? Weren't you about to break up with her?" He had been with her longer than usual, but surely he wasn't in love with a woman who was snootier than our own mothers, was he?

"That's the problem. I wasn't." He sighed.

"Wait, hold the phone. You actually like this woman?" I knew incredulity dripped from my words, but come on. This was the person who'd looked down her nose at me. Any woman who couldn't appreciate a Santa-themed, Hawaiian-print shirt wouldn't do well with Jake.

I wasn't the only one who wore them, usually. Come to think of it, Jake hadn't been wearing his Hawaiian-print shirts lately. Did he really like Sonya enough to change up his wardrobe?

"I *love* this woman." He sounded like a lovelorn fool. Since when did Jake Anderson trip over himself for any woman?

I had to tread carefully here. If Jake really did care for this woman, then I needed to be understanding. At least until he met the next hot chick he'd date for a month and throw away with the magazines.

"I'm sorry, buddy, really I am. Did you two fight?"

"No, she dumped me for another man. I don't think I'm rich enough for her." Jake wasn't Trump-family rich, but he did come from money and made a decent living on his own. He'd never be a billionaire, but his family did have millions. How anyone could thumb their nose at that sort of money was beyond me.

"Whoa, did she actually say those words?" I couldn't believe any woman come right out and say a man didn't have enough money for her needs.

He paused a moment before sighing. Then Jake admitted she didn't come right out and say it. "What she said was that we had different goals and I wasn't motivated to work enough for her lifestyle. I read between the lines."

"Then you're better off without her. She sounds like the type of woman who was only interested in you for the money."

"I don't care. I would have spent it all on her if she'd stayed with me." When he moaned, that was it.

"Listen up, man. You gotta get her out of your mind. Let's go out and you can meet someone better." I knew once he met another woman, Sonya would be forgotten. He was probably only upset because she'd done the dumping and not him.

"No, I don't want anyone but Sonya."

Was that crying I heard over the phone? Was Jake Anderson, star football player and total ladies' man, crying over a woman? "I'm coming over. You better be dressed and ready to go out."

When I arrived, Jake wasn't ready. He was sitting at his breakfast table, dishes everywhere, crying over nothing. I could have kicked myself for not talking to him about this crazy woman sooner. I could see at the party that she was no good for him, but I was too wrapped up in my own affairs to remember to speak to him about her. In fact, I hadn't seen him since the party.

Normally we met up once a week for at least a meal, and several times a month for golf or a game of football if enough of the guys were available. Half of our high school team was married with kids. The other half worked hard like we did. But we always found time to meet up. Well, those who stayed nearby, at least.

"Corbin, help me. I need to get Sonya back." Jake's eyes were downcast and blurry with unshed tears. His dark hair was messy, but not in the stylish way. It was obvious he hadn't run a comb through his hair in days. And when I sniffed, I could tell he hadn't showered, either.

"Alright, Jake. You aren't going to attract any attention, except maybe rodents, without a shower. Come on, first thing's first—get yourself cleaned up. Then we'll go out to eat. I doubt you've even eaten a decent meal the past few days."

Jake shook his head. "No, I couldn't eat anything. Not when my heart is breaking."

"I'm going to break something else if you don't get off your sorry butt and get yourself cleaned up," I barked at him, and he finally looked me in the eye.

"Corbin, what am I gonna do?"

"Jake, you're going to listen to me and shower. After you're dressed, we're going out for dinner." I crossed my arms over my chest and stared him down, just like coach used to do when we were being obstinate.

It got him moving, slowly. But he did shower and put on clean clothes.

Over a meal at TGI Fridays, I got him to open up a bit more about Sonya. I hadn't realized they'd dated for almost two months. How did I not know that?

Work had been hectic these past few months, and then Millie came back into my life. But that was no reason to ignore my best friend. Jake had earned that title after Millie turned her back on me in high school, and he'd stayed at the top of my list for the past fourteen years.

I had to do better by him.

"Jake, I had no idea you cared so much for Sonya. I'm sorry it didn't work out with her."

I waited for him to reply, but he stared mutely at his plate. The woman must have put a hex on my friend, for this was not the man I'd known since high school.

He took a few more bites of his steak without comment.

"How about we play a round of golf tomorrow? I'll call and see if we can get a tee time." I had some work to do, but my friend needed me. While his family weren't members at my country club, I could bring a guest. Jake and I took each other to our country clubs for golfing all the time. He knew almost as many people at the Corona Springs Estates and Golf Club as I did.

"Sure, if you want." Jake's lack of enthusiasm had me really worried. Would it help to introduce him to a new woman? Or did he really have feelings for Sonya? Feelings that needed time to erode.

The next day was sunny but not too hot, which was a blessing since we couldn't get a time until two in the afternoon. But we made it work. I brought along a cooler of water and Coke, along with a few snacks.

After the first three holes, Jake began to show interest in our game. He even poked fun at me when I hit a ball into the trees. That was my first double-bogey in a long while, but worth it to see the smile that spread over Jake's face.

By the time we hit the tenth hole, he was even flirting with the girl who ran the drink cart. The clubs always employed young, single, pretty women to drive the drink cart. It somehow worked to get men to buy more drinks than they normally would. Even though I had plenty of Coke for us, Jake bought a Coke from the girl, Tina, just so he could flirt with her.

"I knew playing a round of golf would get you out of your funk." I looked back over my shoulder and noticed the drink girl was still smiling at Jake. I also noticed that he held a piece of paper in his hands. "Ah, a phone number."

He nodded and smiled. The first real smile of the day. "Yeah, but I'm not gonna use it."

"Why not? She's pretty. And she seems interested." Jake had once told me that was really all he needed in a woman.

"But she's not Sonya." Jake put the piece of paper in his pants pocket and got back in the cart so we could move to the next hole.

"Give it a few days, then see how you feel." Hopefully he'd be over Sonya enough by then to call the girl. Even if he did nothing more than call her, at least it was a start.

"Say, I'm going to attend the July 4th picnic here at the club. You wanna join me?" I intentionally left off the fact that I was also going to escort Millie. I didn't need Jake to think he was going to be a third wheel. But if he could be his normal self, he'd meet many young women who'd like to date him. The attention alone might be enough to make him forget about Sonya.

I guess it was a good thing Sonya had broken up with Jake the way she did. Now Jake would be able to see that she was a no-good, money-hungry she-devil. Hopefully he'd never go back to her, even if she came crawling back to him. While this hurt my friend, it might also be the best thing to ever happen to him. Maybe now he'd be nicer to the women he dated when he broke up with them.

From what I'd heard, he didn't always break up in a nice way. There were even a few he ghosted. No one deserved that.

Jake shrugged. "Maybe. When do I need to let you know?"

"By Sunday. I need to let the club know how many I'll be bringing so they can have an accurate count for the food. I heard they're going to bury a pig as well as grill salmon." I loved it when they grilled fish of any sort. I wasn't the best cook, and fish was one of those meals I always messed up. I either overcooked it and it turned out rubbery, or I undercooked it and it was cool and fishy tasting. Forget about seasoning. That was something I couldn't seem to get right, either.

Now give me some beef and I could season, grill, or bake it to perfection. Cooking red meat must have been one of those things that was ingrained in all men. I didn't know a single man who couldn't cook up a good cut of beef or pork.

It probably came from our days as cavemen.

Chapter 18

Millie

The big day had come and I was nervous. More than usual for a date. I knew how important today was to not only my reputation, but to my family's. And to the Deeks. They were going out on a limb having Corbin take me to my first public event since I'd sat on the plate of cake.

For most, that incident would have meant nothing. People would have laughed and it might have come up now and then at parties. But for me, it was just another in a long line of accidents—or *incidents*, as I preferred to call them.

And considering that the cake debacle had happened so quickly after the Christmas Crazy incident, well...let's just say people would be watching me.

All I could say was that I was glad today was about the birth of our nation. I loved celebrating the Fourth of July. Each summer I looked forward to the food, the fireworks, and the company of friends.

While this picnic at the club would take place on a Saturday every year, it didn't always take place on the Fourth of July. This year, it was the second of July. On Monday, my family and the Deeks would gather at Corbin's parents' house for a very small barbecue. I almost never had an issue when it was a small group.

But today we were going to be surrounded by several hundred people, and I would have to be on my best behavior. Since it was outdoors, I decided a flowing summer dress and sandals would be best. Heels could make me trip so easily while walking on uneven ground. I knew my mother would be dressed in heels, but I wasn't my mother. And thankfully, she no longer dressed me. Although, she would if I allowed it.

I chose my dress for today. It might have been a bit loud, but it suited me and my mood. The bodice was tight and sleeveless while the skirt flowed out and went down to my calves. It was red, white, and blue for the occasion. Fireworks burst forth across the skirt while the top was a solid red. I felt pretty and patriotic at the same time. I found these cute and comfortable strappy sandals which were red with a silver star right above the strap that went between my big toe and the next one. Perfect for a patriotic day, or any day really.

When the doorbell rang, my heart began beating triple-time. This was it. Other than one quick phone call to discuss details, I hadn't seen or heard from Corbin since he came by last week. I found that I'd missed him, which was strange since we had barely even begun talking again.

I wasn't quite sure if this was a date or an assignment for Corbin. He was the one who'd called and asked me. And we set the time for him to pick me up—noon today—but he'd never said the word *date*.

I hated not knowing if it was a date or not. Only time would tell how he felt about our outing.

With purse in hand, I stopped at the front door with my fingers on the knob and took a deep breath before opening it. "Corbin..."

I was about to say it was good to see him, but it wasn't Corbin.

Instead, Jake Anderson stood at my door. Corbin's best friend. A guy who dated any pretty thing in a skirt. I'd describe him as a man-whore, but word on the street was that he never dated anyone long enough to sleep with them.

I double-checked the time; it was noon—the time Corbin and I had agreed on. "Jake, what can I do for you?"

He grinned and his beautiful, sparkling white teeth shone. "Hiya, beautiful. I'm here to pick you up."

My brow furrowed, and I wasn't sure if this was a dream, or what? A nightmare? "Where's Corbin?"

"At his place. He asked me to pick you up and head over to get him. He's a little behind on work and needed the extra time to finish up an email or some nonsense." Jake waved a hand in the air.

"Ah, so you're coming with us?" I didn't want to sound unhappy, but...well...I had hoped it would be just Corbin and me.

He shrugged. "I guess. Are you ready?" His demeanor changed, and I could tell he'd noticed I wasn't too happy about this.

I hoped I hadn't hurt his feelings.

I pulled the door closed behind me and locked it. So, this was *not* a date then. He'd sent his friend to pick me up without even calling me or texting me the change in plans. I didn't know if I should be upset, hurt, or relieved it wasn't a date.

Was that relief filling my chest? I thought I might be happy this was just a friendly outing, but couldn't be sure. Either way, I was disappointed that Corbin couldn't be bothered to let me know he'd sent an alternate to pick me up. I mean, I barely knew Jake Anderson.

However, I needed to be the society woman I was raised to be. And showing any disappointment in the new arrangements just wasn't done. So it was time to put on my mask.

By the time I turned around, I had a real smile on my face. Jake and I had never been close, but he was Corbin's best friend. I needed to get along with this guy.

"I like your shirt. Very patriotic." He had on a Hawaiian-print shirt that basically matched me. It was red with flags and fireworks interspersed with red, white, and blue flowers. If I was a little loud, he was screaming at the world.

There was something calming about his shirt, even though it would probably be the loudest shirt at the party. However, I still had to see Corbin's shirt. Even though we hadn't spoken in fourteen years, it didn't mean I hadn't noticed his penchant for loud, Hawaiian-print shirts.

Jake seemed to notice my change in attitude and his smile reappeared when we got in his SUV. He drove a large black Cadillac Escalade. He didn't need a vehicle this large since he was single, but it was a statement car.

Who was I to judge? I drove a pretty little convertible Audi TT. I didn't buy it new, but it was in excellent shape. It was red with a black soft top, and I captured a lot of attention when I drove it with the top down. I guessed I, too, drove a statement vehicle. Although mine had probably cost a quarter of what his did.

Jake had third-row seating, a moon roof, heated and cooled seats, along with a plethora of other extras. "Is that a DVD system?" I pointed to the screen on the dashboard between us. "Have you ever watched a movie while you were driving?"

He chuckled. "Yes, it's a DVD player, but no, I don't watch movies while I drive. I got it more for when I'm tailgating than anything else."

"That must be nice. Does it also have a TV connection, so you can watch the game from the parking lot?" I knew he and the guys went to a lot of football games; it only made sense, since they'd all played in high school. And a few even went on to play college ball. None of them were drafted into the NFL, but one did play in a foreign league over in Europe. He'd only played for two years, if memory served.

"No, I don't have an antenna to get the signal. But I suppose I could use my laptop and then send the image to the DVD screen on my car? But my laptop's screen is bigger, so that wouldn't work too well." He pointed to the nine-inch screen covering the center console. "Besides, we all prefer to go into the game once we're done tailgating."

"Who's your date today?" I'd never seen him without a date at the society events. And I didn't remember if he had a new girlfriend, or if she was someone I'd met. I couldn't keep up with women in his life, nor did I want to. Jake never dated the sort of woman I'd be friends with, anyway.

He cleared his throat. "I'm not seeing anyone at the moment. Which is why Corbin invited me to join the two of you."

If I didn't know any better, I'd think Corbin was trying to set me up with Jake. But there was no way Jake would want to go out with me, even for one date. And I would never want to date a man who changed his women almost as often as he changed his underwear.

"That was nice of him. This should be fun." Not really, but I was taught to be a nice hostess. Maybe having Jake along would help to keep me out of trouble? Four eyes were better than two, right?

When we pulled up to Corbin's loft condo, I looked to Jake. "I'll go get him if you want to keep the car going and the A/C running." I grinned at him. It was a hot day. If we could keep in an air-conditioned car a little bit longer, it might help to make the afternoon easier to deal with.

Sedately, I walked up to the door. Even though I knew we were running a little late, I wasn't about to do anything to cause me to sweat before we arrived at the party. It was very important to come into the celebration looking my best.

Before I could bring my fist up to knock on Corbin's door, it opened. A smiling, handsome man greeted me.

"Why hello, beautiful." Corbin leaned over to hug me.

I hugged him back and felt the edges of my lips curve in greeting. When he pulled back, I checked out his shirt. He had on a midnight-blue shirt with splotches of fireworks in various colors all over. There were a few flags waving in the wind behind the palm trees on his shirt, too.

"And here I thought Jake's shirt would be the loudest." I couldn't help the giggle that escaped my lips.

Corbin frowned, then looked down at the shirt he'd paired with khaki shorts. "What? You don't like it?"

I waved a hand in front of me. "No, actually I do like it." I bit my lower lip, considering my next words. "But something tells me your mother and mine won't."

He grinned and raised his brows. "I know. It's great, isn't it?"

I nodded and did a twirl. "Do you think my mother will approve of my dress?"

Corbin whistled and motioned for me to do another twirl. "I love it. I don't care what the moms have to say, I think you look wonderful and very patriotic. But I'm surprised. I thought you weren't into the summer holidays?"

I waited for him to shut and lock his door before we walked back to Jake's waiting SUV. "I said I wasn't doing Christmas in July. I never said I wasn't going to celebrate the birth of our great nation."

"Touché. I'm glad you're having fun with today." Corbin opened the front passenger-side door for me.

When we were seated, I looked back over the seat. "I'm having fun now. Let's wait and see what happens at the country club."

Chapter 19

Corbin

Millie was magnificent. Her auburn hair had been pulled back on the sides and braided against her head while the rest of it cascaded down her back. She wore large sunglasses that curved to the bottom of her bangs so that most of her face was covered, except the lower portion.

I wished she hadn't covered her eyes. Now all I could see were her lips. Full, pink lips that I wanted to kiss. I couldn't think like this. It was a good thing I'd brought Jake along with us. Having him near would help keep me in line.

"Who's ready for some salmon?" Food—that would take my mind off the beauty standing tall next to me.

We had been here for close to an hour now and there hadn't been any mishaps. So far Millie hadn't tripped on her own toes, nothing was placed on her seat before she could sit down, and no food had found its way down the front of her dress. Things were looking up. But we had thought that same exact thing right before Mrs. Green put her cake underneath Millie. I had promised the moms I would take care of Millie and keep her out of trouble, and that was exactly what I was going to do.

Even Jake had offered to help me keep Millie accident-free. Which was a very nice offer, and a surprising observation by a man who only seemed to notice women if they were his *type*. And Millie most certainly was *not* his type.

Not because Millie wasn't beautiful, for she really was quite spectacular. But because she wasn't the sort to flirt with Jake and be his arm candy. That was it—Millie wasn't arm candy, she was long-term girlfriend material. Maybe even wife material.

Whoa, where'd that thought come from?

No, I couldn't think that sort of thought. Not about the person who had been my best friend for my entire childhood. Nope, wasn't gonna go there. She needed my help this summer, and I promised I'd get her out of this stupid mess.

But really, why was it so bad? I got the high school pool incident. That was really bad for a teenager, and the way everyone back in school gossiped, but today? It wasn't like Millie was sleeping with a married man or stole anything.

Okay, so if the incident with the purse ever became public knowledge, that might be gossip-worthy. But her falling in the mud? That shouldn't have been a big deal. But there was a news van there and they'd gotten it all on tape. That had to be the reason it became such fodder for the gossip mill.

Thankfully, sitting on a piece of cake didn't last long; Melinda getting caught with a councilman took all attention off of everyone else. My mom said she heard that someone's daughter was caught shoplifting—*actually* shoplifting. Stealing with intent to steal. But she couldn't be sure since everyone was focused on Melinda and Ron.

Hopefully, even if something bad did happen today it wouldn't be noticed. I could hear people still talking about Melinda and the Corona city councilman. I doubted that bit of juicy news would be preempted any time soon.

Poor Melinda. Actually, scratch that. I felt sorry for her kids. It was a good thing they were out of school for the summer. Bullies would have a field day with this sort of ammunition.

"Uh-oh," I said sotto voce to Millie. "Looks like Jake has his next target."

Millie followed my gaze and giggled. "I should have known he'd find someone today. When he told me he wasn't seeing anyone, I was shocked. I guess he just needed a venue to find a new main squeeze?"

I held back a snort at her apt description of my best buddy. "Yeah, it was only a matter of time."

"Why do you think he never stays with anyone for long?" Millie asked.

The way Millie tilted her head to one side and looked at Jake had me wondering if she wanted to be his next conquest. When a pain shot through my heart like a knife, I worried that the green-eyed monster might be coming for a visit. I had to turn away from Jake.

"Uh, I don't think Jake is ready for commitment. His parents divorced when he was a kid and it was pretty nasty. So he hasn't wanted to have anything to do with marriage and kids." I considered Millie for a moment and wondered what she thought about having her own family.

"Yeah, I can see that in him." Millie turned back toward me and frowned. "What's wrong?" Then she proceeded to look all around herself and down at the ground by her feet.

"Don't worry, you haven't stepped in anything, yet." I chuckled.

"Hardy har har. But thanks." She sucked in her bottom lip and considered me. "Something is off with you. What's going on?"

"Why do you say that?" I really didn't want her knowing what I was thinking at that very moment. I would have scared her off, probably for good this time. And the last thing I wanted to do was lose her friendship again.

"Oh, I don't know. You look contemplative, or frustrated? I'm not really sure what your different facial expressions mean anymore." Millie motioned with her hand in a circle in front of my face. "It's been a while since we spoke. But back in high school I would have thought you were thinking about something pretty serious. What's up?"

"Good thing my name's not Chuck, right?" That old joke just flowed out without me even thinking. I started to feel that we might be getting our mojo back.

Unfortunately, Millie was taking a drink of her iced tea when I said it. Liquid spewed out of her nose and she started coughing.

I felt rotten. I was supposed to help her keep from making any scenes. While choking on a drink wasn't any big deal—certainly not gossip-worthy—it was just one more thing to add to her list of klutzy incidents.

She did have a napkin in her hand and was able to cover her mouth rather quickly. I gave her mine as well, and in no time she had it all under control.

"What?" She chuckled. "You remembered?"

"Of course I did. I haven't forgotten anything, Millie." I took a step closer and put my hand on her arm.

Her cheeks turned a pretty shade of pink. "Really? Even the pool?"

I sighed. "I'm so sorry, but I'll never forget how beautiful you were that day."

"What about the rest? How I looked like a drowned rat after I got out of the pool." Millie's eyebrows furrowed and her lips parted. "Jake helped me out that day, didn't he? I totally forgot about that."

And again, the stupid green-eyed monster reared its ugly head. I was the one who'd saved her from drowning, but she remembered Jake helping her out of the pool?

"Millie, even all wet you were still the most beautiful girl there." I wanted to say more, like remind her how I'd saved her, but then she'd probably remember that I was the one who threw the football at her chest.

"Thank you for helping me to the side of the pool. I don't think I ever thanked you for the help."

She hadn't. Instead, she'd yelled at me that day and ran away.

I wanted to say it was my pleasure, but that didn't sound right. Not at all. So I just nodded. "Say, why don't we find a table to sit at and get a fresh drink? I promise, no jokes until you finish your next tea."

The tinkling sound that came from her lips was like music to my ears. "Sounds great, thanks." She gave me one of her sweet smiles, the kind that sent tendrils of delight through my veins.

That felt much better than a visit from the green-eyed monster. I wasn't sure why I had an issue with Millie thinking fondly of Jake. It wasn't like Jake would ever ask her out. And I seriously doubted she'd say yes to him, anyways. But jealousy had been what I'd felt. Maybe bringing Jake on this date was a bad idea.

Chapter 20

Millie

Man, did I ever wish Jake hadn't joined us today. I know, I know, it wasn't a date. But still, I had hoped it would have turned into one. Although, Jake did disappear with some woman. I didn't recognize her, but there were so many guests at the club today, who knew where that woman actually lived? It might very well have been her first time here.

Would Jake forget about us? Nah, he knew he had driven all three of us to the party. He wouldn't dare leave us stranded here, would he? Wait, that was just one more negative thought I needed to banish.

This past week I had started a new daily devotional by Joyce Meyer. She wrote about how we could change our negative attitudes and feelings by just changing our thoughts. Thinking positive thoughts instead of negative on a regular basis could change our entire attitude.

Focusing on God instead of the bad things in life was one such way to improve my thought life, and my attitude. And since I needed an attitude adjustment, as well as a positive thought life, I had decided to give this new concept a try.

Jake wasn't going to leave us stranded. And if for some reason our ride did leave, it wouldn't be difficult to get a ride back to my place. Corbin lived closer to the country club, so we could share a ride to his place and then he could drive me home. Okay, problem solved. Well, if there was a future problem, I'd solved it.

"Today turned out a bit nicer than expected, didn't it?" Okay, so my conversation skills need a little work. Talking about the weather is one of those topics that can help get a good conversation going. Right?

"It really did. I love this cool breeze coming over the mountains from the beach." Guess I wasn't the only one who was interested in our weather. Corbin looked around and grinned. Then he pointed. "Look, our parents are all watching us."

While he grinned, I groaned. All I needed was a play by play from my mother. Tomorrow she'd have some reason to call me, and then she'd tell me everything she had noticed. And she always saw something wrong.

"Why don't we go say hi?" Corbin took my hand and we walked across the lawn to where the picnic tables had been set up for this event.

His hand felt so right in mine. *Stop that.* I had to remind myself that we were only friends. Today wasn't even a date, for pity's sake. *Only friends, only friends, only friends.* I prayed that if I told myself enough times that he wasn't interested in me romantically, my heart would get the memo and stop beating so hard whenever he got near me, or spoke to me, or shoot, even looked at me. *Gah!* I was such a sappy chick.

The moment we were close to my parents, I put on a happy face and greeted them.

"Millie, your dress, it's so..." My mom, the fashion critic. She had wanted to choose my dress for me, but I wanted something I felt comfortable in. And I happened to love this dress.

"I know, isn't it awesome?" Corbin winked at me and then turned his smile to my parents.

"Well, you two do match." Mrs. Deeks had to add her two cents.

I looked to Corbin and grinned. I knew his parents wouldn't be happy with his choice of shirt. So I guess we did make a good pair. We'd both worn what made us happy, and in the process upset both sets of parents. Not that either of us would want to make the 'rents unhappy, but, well, I'd say it was a bonus.

My mom was forever complaining about my wardrobe. Which was why I went to the stupid dress shop last month to begin with. I only wanted to please her, and I ended up being the big story of the night. Or was it month? Certainly I was the headliner for at least a week.

"Well, we have others to greet. It was nice seeing you both. Catch ya later." Corbin took my hand again and led me far away from our parents.

I could have kissed him. Not that I would have in this setting, but you know, it was totally something that crossed my mind. And only because he'd rescued us both so easily, and quickly. The idea of kissing him had nothing to do with the fact that I couldn't take my eyes off of his mouth every time he smiled. And he smiled a lot.

Was my nose growing? I might have to stop lying to myself.

"That was a close one." Corbin pulled me around the corner of one of the large pop-up tents they'd rented for today's events. Inside, they had seating for those who wanted to be out of the sun. The only downside, no breeze.

"Thank you. I didn't know if I could take their scrutiny any longer." The moment Mrs. Deeks mentioned that Corbin and I matched, all I could think of was how cute we looked together. I knew Mrs. Deeks well enough to know it wouldn't take long before she had us married with two point five kids, a dog, and a white picket fence. If she went there, it would break my heart to hear Corbin shut it all down. And he would.

To be honest, I probably would have as well. Sure, I still had some feelings for the hottie, but thoughts of marriage? I hadn't had those fantasies since I was seventeen. And even then, it was a fleeting thought. More like when girls wrote their name out and used the last name of the boy they liked. Something silly we all did, but knew deep down it would never end that way.

Now, I needed to get my head on straight and just enjoy today. If I spent too much time thinking about us as a possible couple, I'd end up doing something stupid, like driving a golf cart into a water trap. Now that would be gossip-worthy. And probably something I'd do.

"How about an old-fashioned shaved ice?" Corbin pointed to the area that held a couple of pop-ups with food vendors.

Most events would have hired out food trucks and then placed them in various spots around the property. But not a country club. A food truck was too common, even though some of the most well-known chefs had food trucks at one time or another. And there were apps designed to help foodies find the best food trucks in town, all over the country. Nope, our country club was run by people still stuck in the sixties, when everyone called food trucks *roach coaches*.

Hey board of regents, there's a *huge* difference between a roach coach and a fifteen-dollar burger from a gourmet food truck. I even followed several social media accounts where the truck had its own account. Those were my favorite.

Well, second favorite.

My favorite social media accounts were ones set up by animals. I just loved to see a cute baby elephant loving up on its momma. Or the latest craze, cow cuddling. There was a ranch in Montana with a B&B where the guests could cuddle Scottish Highland cows, or kews, as it's pronounced. So cool! Now that everything was back open, I might have to put them on my list of places to visit on my next vacation.

Actually, if things didn't improve around here, it might behoove me to go find a cow to cuddle. I heard it was very therapeutic.

"I'd love a shaved ice." I followed Corbin and thought about the last time I'd had one. "You know, I don't think I've had one in at least a decade. Have you?"

We spent our time in line discussing the merits of the flavors and colors one could ask for from this vendor. And we decided to try a variety of flavors and share. That way we could taste-test more.

I just prayed I wouldn't spill anything down the front of my pretty dress. Although, the red syrup probably wouldn't be too noticeable. "Maybe I should just get a cherry shaved ice and play it safe?"

"No way. We're gonna enjoy today. We'll just pay attention to what we're doing and you won't spill anything." He glared at me.

Corbin had been right—the blue razzleberry flavor was the best. And the worst was the rockin' greenade. I should have known a puke-green color would result in a puke-green taste.

"Corbin? Uh, is that Jake?" I slapped Corbin's shoulder when he didn't respond. We were standing in a circle of his high school buddies. They were all laughing and recounting their glory days when I noticed someone wearing a loud, patriotic Hawaiian-print shirt. It looked a lot like the one Jake had been wearing. And from the back, the guy looked like Jake.

Except for the lobster bisque pouring down his dark-brown head.

The guys all broke out in hysterical laughter.

"If it wasn't you, Millie, it had to be someone you knew," Mark Gonzalez, one of the high school jocks, bellowed.

Corbin shook his head. "Nope, that's not Jake."

I took a closer look and realized this guy wasn't nearly as tall as Jake. But from behind, he could have been a body double. Well, if you didn't count the height difference.

I was just glad it wasn't someone I knew. Someone else and their family and friends could be the center of attention. But I was curious why he had a bowl of soup over his head. That lobster bisque was fantastic. What a waste of good food.

"Then who is it?" I asked our group.

All heads shook in denial. No one else seemed to know the poor schmuck, either.

A blond woman who couldn't have been much over twenty-one walked out of a stand of trees, brandishing a soup ladle.

Who walks around a copse of trees with a soup ladle? Did I just walk into an episode of *The Twilight Zone*? I could swear there was one that started out this way, wasn't there? If not, there should've been.

The heebie-jeebies crept over my skin and the hair on my arms stood at attention. "Corbin? Wha...what's going on?" I hiccuped partway through my question.

"Uh, don't ask me. But I think the gossip is somehow going to change to this poor couple."

Two degrees of separation now existed between me and my latest snafu. Could I hope for more? No, scratch that. I hated that anyone else had to suffer just so I could escape notice.

Mark's head moved back and forth, and the spot between his eyes crinkled. Then he pointed to another spot. "Jake?"

I looked and found Jake with a beautiful blonde. However, it wasn't the one he'd left us for earlier in the day. He was with a new one. Wait, hold the phone. I took another look at the woman with the ladle and felt a bubble of laughter well up from within.

"Wasn't that"—I pointed to the woman with the overly large soup spoon—"the woman Jake walked off with earlier? Who's he with now?"

Corbin scratched his head. "This is getting strange. Come on, let's go see Jake and find out what's happening."

"Corbin, thank goodness." Jake walked up to us. "Today is one of those days where you think you're living in a dream, but then you look around and realize it's real life." He shook his head.

"What happened? I thought you were with that other chick?" I pointed to the woman giving the Jake lookalike a death glare.

"Yeah, I was. But then that guy came up and took her away. I think they're dating or something? I don't know. But they have a food tent here. Good soup." Jake shrugged.

"Uh-huh. So then why does he look so much like you? And why is she threatening him?" I asked.

Jake winced. "I think they had a fight."

"Uh, duh, Sherlock. But why?" Corbin deadpanned. Then he proceeded to slap the back of Jake's head.

Just what I was thinking about doing, but didn't have the courage to do.

Jake sniggered. "Oh, I don't know. Maybe her guy was jealous of me? I am better looking than he is. And my taste in clothes is definitely better."

"Oh, brother. What, are we back in high school again?" It was funny, but there was no way I was going to let Jake know that he was sort of a comedian. The fact that the two men were practically dressed in identical shirts must have slipped past Jake's notice.

The woman next to Jake laughed. "Actually, I think they did fight over you. But something tells me that the woman used you to make her boyfriend jealous."

I looked at the new girl and then back to Jake and raised my brows. Jake just stood there like an idiot, grinning. I cleared my throat and then nodded in the direction of the woman, who took two steps closer to Jake.

Jake looked between us. "Oh, I'm sorry. Millie, this is Bethany. Bethany, this is Millie Milan, Corbin's date for today."

I waved. "Hi. Nice to meet you."

"And this is Corbin Deeks." Jake motioned to the man at my side.

I noticed that while Jake had introduced us using our full names, he'd left off Bethany's last name. Which made me think he'd only just met her.

"Do you know the happy couple?" I motioned with my head toward the arguing couple who were attracting more attention than they needed. Especially if they were part of the catering services for the day.

"Actually, I do." Bethany sighed. "The guy, he's my brother, Aiden. And the woman, Alexandra, is his girlfriend. They've been off and on for a while now. Sorry for the display." She cringed.

When Corbin turned to look at me, the sparkle in his eye spoke volumes. We used to be on the same exact wavelength, and I think we still were. His look told me he was thinking the same thing I was: Jake really knew how to pick 'em. First, he picked up a girl who was dating a guy that could easily be his body double, except for the whole height issue. Jake had at least four inches on the guy, if not more. Then, he picked up a girl who was the *sister* of that same guy. Kinda creepy if you ask me. While I didn't have a brother, I'd never be interested in a man who looked like my brother, or any other member of my family.

I had to bite the inside of my cheek to keep from laughing, while Corbin had to cough to hide his laugh.

Jake wasn't going to live this down for a while.

The lobster bisque incident was all anyone could talk about for the next hour. And I was already tired of it. I felt bad for the couple. Sure, they shouldn't have aired their dirty laundry at a country club event, especially one they were working, but come on. Give them a break.

Corbin rolled his eyes when the couple at the table next to us started talking about the soup debacle. "Too bad, that bisque was lovely. I was hoping to get the recipe."

"Come on." Corbin stood and put his hand out for me. "Let's go for a walk before the fireworks start."

"As long as we talk about something besides lobster bisque." I stood up and took his hand.

He chortled. "Deal."

Once we were away from the crowd of gossipers, Corbin looked at me. "So, what did you think of the fish?"

I rolled my eyes.

"What? I meant the salmon. What did you think I meant? Surely not the forbidden topic." He looked around with wide eyes, then put a finger to his lips in the hush symbol.

He was too cute. "Fine, the salmon was really good. Cooked to perfection. Too bad I couldn't go back for seconds of the soup." I grinned.

We both laughed, and the tension that had surrounded us since the incident ebbed away. I was finally relaxing and enjoying my time with Corbin.

"What an interesting first date to have."

Corbin's statement stopped me in my tracks. "What do you mean?" There was no way he was talking about this being *our* first date. Was he?

"Well, I sent my friend to pick you up, then said friend caused an uproar with a couple who were working here, and apparently the guy's little sister." Corbin looked back over his shoulder. "You don't think that girl was underage, do you?"

My head was spinning. He was all over the place right now and I couldn't keep up. "Wait, roll back. Date? Did you say we were on a date today?"

Confusion covered his face. "Yes, don't you think it's a date? I mean, I did call you up and ask you out."

This was one of those universal confusions as old as age. No wonder the cavemen just banged their women over the head before throwing them over their shoulder and going out. Though, while it was much easier to know the situation, that wouldn't work well today. Ewww.

Today, men were supposed to use the word "date." Sadly, they rarely did. So us women never knew if they were intending it to be a friends' thing or a date thing. And the fact that he sent his friend to pick me up without even calling to tell me, well, that said it all. Alright, fine, I was still a bit miffed over that part.

I mean, come on, how hard is it to pick up your cell phone and type in a few words? All he had to do was write, *Sorry, running late. Jake's picking you up.* How hard would that have been? It wouldn't have even taken a minute out of his time to do that.

"But you never mentioned the word date. And you sent your proxy to pick me up." I put my hands on my hips.

"I was running late."

I shook my head. "You didn't even bother to call me and let me know some guy I barely knew was coming to get me."

"Oh, come on. You know Jake."

"No, I don't know Jake." The way his name came out almost sounded like Jack. Which had me smiling. I couldn't help it. Darn this man, I couldn't even stay mad at him anymore. What had happened? When he smiled, a little dimple formed in his left cheek and it was so adorable.

If only that cute dimple would have helped his cause back in high school. I knew I'd missed out on so many great times over these past fourteen years. Maybe that was why I couldn't stay mad at him? My subconscious was rearing her ugly head and wasn't going to let me ruin any more time with Corbin.

Corbin smirked. "You don't know Jack? Really?"

"Ugh, sometimes I wonder how we can really be in our thirties." I shook my head and laughed. "Okay, let's get real. Is this a date?"

He nodded. "Oh yeah, it's a date. Fourteen years too late, but it's still a date."

"Huh?" How was I so confused today?

"I wanted to ask you out fourteen years ago. I tried asking you to prom, but you refused my calls and sent back my letters." The sad puppy dog eyes Corbin gave me broke my heart. Until I remembered who he'd gone with.

"Yeah, going to prom with Melinda had to have been tough." I rolled my eyes. He didn't have to tell me who he took—she'd told me. Plenty of times.

Corbin's head shook so violently, I was afraid it would fall off. "No way, no how, nuh-uh. I know she spread rumors about us, but I never took her to prom."

I put my hands on my hips, remembering the gossip that went around the Monday after prom. "I know, you took her to a hotel instead." I'd gotten him there. I bet he had no idea that I knew what he'd done.

Gross. Even if I had forgiven him after that, there was no way on God's green Earth I would have gotten near him with a ten-foot pole.

"You believed that lie? Really? I thought you knew me better than that." Corbin's shoulders sagged, and he kicked at a small rock sitting in front of his shoe.

"Wait, you didn't have sex with Melinda on prom night?"

"No, I've never touched the ska...girl." It sounded like he was about to use my nickname for Melinda. Corbin was too much of a gentleman to use such a word, at least in front of a lady.

Now I felt awful.

"But the entire school talked about it all week after prom. Everyone said the reason neither of you were there was because you took her to the Sleazy 8 Motel on the edge of town that night." I wracked my brain trying to remember any more of the details that went around, but that was all I could remember.

He shook his head. "No. She kept asking me to take her. I think she even bought the tickets for us. But I never once gave her any indication I'd take her. Did you ever see us together at school?"

I didn't think I had, but I figured he'd conquered that like so many others had and moved on. I thought that half the team had slept with her once and moved on. "Did Jake ever sleep with her?"

He laughed so hard, he almost snorted. "No way. Jake might have low standards, but he's not the male slut that most think he is. In fact, I can only remember one guy on the team sleeping with her. He got something from her and the rest of us made a pact to stay far away from her."

"Wait, only one football player slept with her, really?" I scrunched my nose. Maybe she wasn't the high school slut I thought she was.

"Oh, she tried. And she spread a lot of rumors about herself. But no, none of the guys on any of the teams wanted to take a chance on getting an STD, so we all stayed clear. I know, she was a cheerleader, and stereotypes and all that. But honestly, if she was sleeping around, it wasn't with the players."

"Huh. Why would someone spread rumors like that about themselves?" I rubbed my face and shook my head.

"Usually it's because someone doesn't think very highly of themselves." Corbin winced. "And look at her role model. Not a very good home life. And if she hadn't been caught in bed with Ron, I don't think I would have believed it."

"That's really sad." I bit my lip and felt tears prick the backs of my eyes. I may not have the best sense of self-worth, but I'd never spread lies about myself. "I think I should pray for her. Sounds like no one else is. And everyone needs someone who'll pray for them."

Chapter 21

Corbin

Wow, Millie was something special. How could she feel such tender emotions for someone who had tormented her for most of her life? Melinda had teased Millie incessantly all through high school. She even spread lies about Millie. And now Millie felt sorry for the woman and even wanted to pray for her.

I felt like a cad. I'd never once prayed for Melinda. Well, unless you counted when I prayed for God to keep her away from me. The girl stalked me in high school. I didn't think she'd ever stab me or anything like that, but I did worry that she'd try to crawl into my bedroom at night. I'd heard stories about freaky chicks who did that. Now I was going to have to pray for her, too. Thanks, God.

The rest of the evening was actually quite nice. Millie even took my hand in hers when we walked back to where everyone gathered for the fireworks. The club had put out various types of chairs for the evening after most of the food vendors pulled their tents down and left. All that was left from catering were four tents. Two housed various types of drinks, including hot cocoa, and the other two had desserts.

"How about we sit in one of those Adirondack love seats?" I pointed to a white wooden bench built for two and waggled my brows.

Millie lightly slapped my arm and shook her head. "Alright, lover boy. Let's get one before they're gone."

When we walked over to the seat and sat down, Millie rubbed her hands on her bare arms. The sun was setting and the temperature had taken a pretty drastic dip, especially for July.

I stood up. "How about I get you a blanket and some hot cocoa?"

The tender look she gave me sent my blood pressure skyrocketing. It had been a tumultuous day, but the night was beginning just right.

"And would you mind getting some popcorn while you're up?"

How could I say no to that? I envisioned us sitting very close—so close our shoulders would touch. With the blanket wrapped around our shoulders, drinking hot cocoa and watching the sky explode with color. Then, just before the finale began, we would both reach for the last of the popcorn and I'd entwine our fingers together. Not exactly a *Lady and the Tramp* spaghetti scene, but still a romantic one.

"Be right back." With romantic ideas flowing through my brain, I took off and found a blanket, then got in line for the treats.

By the time I returned, my stomach dropped.

Jake was sitting in my seat. And they were laughing together.

I walked up to them and told myself she was just being nice to my buddy. That was all. "Hey there."

Jake jumped up. "Hey buddy, I was just keeping your girl company. I saw that Ivy League schmuck from the party heading this direction and thought I'd save Millie from a tedious conversation."

"Thank you. I don't think I could have handled another conversation about tennis, or his alma mater." Millie cringed. "I mean, nothing against Harvard. Anyone who graduated from that university is lucky. But I don't need to fall asleep before the fireworks." She giggled and looked at me. Then looked down at the empty spot next to her.

"Thanks, man." I grinned at Jake. He was alright. Perfect wingman. I handed Millie the treats and then wrapped the blanket around her shoulders before I sat down.

"Thank you. I really appreciate it. I should have brought a sweater, but it was so warm earlier I just didn't think about it." She scooched closer to me once I was seated and we both had our treats in hand.

"Aaaannnddd, that's my cue. See ya both after the fireworks." The cheese-eating grin Jake gave me wasn't needed. I'd have to take back the perfect wingman designation; he was too obvious. The perfect wingman would have quietly moved away when the girl was looking directly at me. Then she would have never even noticed he was gone.

"You know, the day may have started out rough, but I'd say the night is getting off to a great start." The moment Millie finished her sentence was the same exact time I heard the whistle of the first fireworks.

We sat close, watching the fireworks. She held the popcorn in her lap and we both held our hot cocoa cups in our other hands. Which left her left hand and my right hand free. Since I was sitting on her left, that meant I could hold her free hand. Which was exactly what I did. When my fingers slid over hers, she was the one who intertwined them. I caught a small smile coming from her out of the corner of my eye.

Neither of us turned our heads from the sky until the display of bursting stars had finished. The crowd all oohed and ahhed at all the right moments. Then, when it was obviously the finale, I squeezed Millie's hand. She returned the gesture and a huge grin spread on my face from ear to ear.

When it was all over, we found Jake not too far from us. He looked between us and still had that stupid cheese-eating smile covering his face. "So kids, ready to head home?" He pulled his key fob out of his pocket. His car had the keyless type of ignition, so there wasn't actually a key there. But the action meant the same—he was ready to leave.

"So," Millie started once we were on our way, "who will you be calling this week, Jake?"

I covered my mouth with my hand to keep from laughing. I had wondered the same thing. For the past few hours I hadn't seen him with anyone, so I wasn't sure who his next date would be with. The woman who had obviously broken up with her longtime boyfriend by throwing a bowl of lobster bisque over his head, or the younger sister of his doppelgänger. Neither were good choices for him. Too much drama.

"Ah, so many choices." Jake gave Millie a quick look. "Why, do you want to be next on my list?"

She laughed. Not a cute little chuckle, either, but the kind that would have spewed liquid all over Jake's car if she had been drinking anything. "Um, no. I don't think I could keep up with you, Jake."

"Yeah, it's probably best that way. I don't want my best buddy to be upset that I stole his new girl." Through the rearview mirror, Jake grinned at me.

If the headrest hadn't been in the way, I would have slapped him up the back of his head. Didn't matter that he was driving. These Cadillacs had excellent crash-test ratings. And besides, we were barely doing five miles an hour trying to get out of the parking lot.

"So, last night." I was on the phone with Millie the day after the picnic. I had just gotten home from church.

"It was a lot of fun. Thank you for asking me out." Millie sounded a bit breathless over the phone.

Was she as excited as I was?

"Sorry, I'm running into the grocery store. I've got nothing for dinner tonight." She chuckled.

"Well, how about I take you out for dinner tonight? And before you ask, it's a date." After the confusion of last night, I wanted to make sure she knew I was in this for more than friendship. Although, I did want her to be my friend again. But this time I wanted our relationship to move to that next level. The one I had hoped for in high school all those years ago.

"A dinner date? Tell me you won't be sending someone else to pick me up," she teased.

I laughed. "I won't ever do that again without letting you know first."

"Deal."

"Great, I'll pick you up at six."

"See you then," she said before hanging up.

Were we really doing this? A date with just the two of us, no one else to help out in case our conversation petered out? It went well last night after I made it clear it was a date, and even better when I suggested I take her home after Jake dropped us off at my place.

Don't worry, I was a perfect gentleman. I didn't even offer her a nightcap. Instead, I went into my house and got the keys to my car and drove her home. Then I walked her up to her front door and gave her a hug goodnight. I wasn't going to ruin this. While yes, I did want to kiss her—oh, how I wanted to kiss the girl!—I was going to take it slow.

I had promised myself I wouldn't ask her out again so soon. I was only calling to see how she was doing. But, okay, I'm weak. What can I say? I had hoped to see her at church, but she must have gone to an earlier service. Our church had two identical Sunday morning services since we were outgrowing our building.

A coffee meetup was all I originally had in mind, but when she mentioned dinner, I didn't even think. I just reacted. And I was glad for it. I was going to have dinner with Millie. I still couldn't believe it.

The only problem was, what was I going to wear?

Chapter 22

Millie

What was I thinking? I had nothing to wear for a date with Corbin. If I'd had time, I would have gone shopping. Well, not gone *out* shopping, but ordered online. The Christmas Crazy was getting worse.

Even at the grocery store there was an entire aisle dedicated to Christmas stuff, just like during the normal Christmas season. But unlike the normal season, people were going crazy over what the grocery store was offering.

It wasn't like they had killer deals on jewelry or clothes. They had wrapping supplies and some decorations. I stopped unloading my groceries and thought back to what I'd seen. Well, okay, they did have some cool stuff there. It looked like a beach-themed Christmas party. As with other items I'd seen this summer, it looked as though manufacturers used what they had created for an Australian Christmas. Which was kinda cool.

"No, not going there. I'm not going to decorate for Christmas in July. And I'm not going to celebrate it, either." Ugh, what was wrong with me? In my hands was a head of green, leafy lettuce. That's what I was talking to. "Alright, head of lettuce, I think it's time I called in the big guns." Which meant I would have to meet up with Jeanie sometime this week and discuss Corbin.

Jeanie and her husband weren't members of the country club, so she wasn't there yesterday. And she probably hadn't heard anything yet about me attending with Corbin. I knew I'd have to tell her. But I didn't think I'd be asking her for dating advice. At least not with Corbin.

Here I was, finally dating the guy I'd wanted back in high school, and I was nervous. Practically on the edge of hysteria, if talking out loud to a head of lettuce was any indication of my mental state.

Back at home, I quickly put away the rest of my groceries, including the talking head of lettuce. Then I went and sat on my couch and panicked. I even thought about calling my mom to ask her for clothing tips. That was desperate thinking.

Instead, I looked at the teddy bear sitting on my chair and picked him up. "Alright, Teddy. It's up to you to help me pick out an outfit for dinner tonight."

I walked us upstairs to my bedroom closet. Then when I looked down at the bear, guilt crept in. "I know, I know. I should call Jeanie now. She'd want to help me with this. But it's Sunday dinner. This is her time with the family."

What was wrong with me? Not only was I talking to a stuffed bear again—this time I was arguing with it.

I threw the teddy bear on my closet floor and pulled my cell out of my back pocket. "Jeanie? Sorry to bother you on a Sunday," I started to say when she screamed in my ear.

"Millie, why didn't you tell me?"

"Tell you what?" Had she already heard about last night? Wow, gossip sure did fly fast around town.

"About everything, including the fact that you're now *dating* Corbin Deeks! I can't believe it. How many times have you two been out already?" Her emphasis on the word "dating" had me wondering what the gossip was.

"Um, we went out yesterday for the first time. I told you I was going to the picnic with him." I knew we had talked about this. She had even asked me if it was a date. I didn't think it was, so I said as much last week when we spoke.

"That's not what I heard."

I did a face-plant on my bed. "What did you hear?" I groaned out once I had turned my face to the side so I could breathe.

"That you and Corbin have been dating for a few weeks now, and it's serious."

"I only just started talking to him a couple of weeks ago. But why am I surprised? It's gossip." Did this mean that Melinda's issues were already forgotten? Did I help her get lowered on the list of juicy tidbits?

"And what was the deal about the lobster eating a man's head off?"

Of course the rumor wasn't accurate, but that was a doozy. So I explained everything that had happened and then asked for her advice about what to wear.

By the time we got off the phone, it was time to dress for my dinner date.

Jeanie helped me to choose a pair of light-blue linen pants with a white-and-blue top with a seashell design on it. I paired the outfit with white flats and topped it all off with a powder-blue light sweater. I didn't have to wear it unless we were out late and it got chilly. A cold front had moved in and the evenings had grown cooler than normal. I wasn't going to complain.

I'd just put the last stroke of mascara on when my doorbell rang. As I walked downstairs, my phone pinged in my hand. When I got to the bottom of the steps I stopped and looked at the message. It was from Corbin.

Sorry, but I'm running late. Jake's picking you up.

"What? I thought this was a dinner date. Ugh." I knew who was at the door. I really didn't want a third wheel for a dinner date. My hand dropped to my side and I went to let Jake in.

"Hey…" I stopped dead in my tracks. Then I burst out laughing. "Okay, that was good."

Standing at my front door was not Jake, but Corbin. I had forgotten how much he loved to pull practical jokes. Inside I was laughing, but outside I had decided to not let him know he'd gotten to me.

"Come on in, I just need to grab my purse." I opened the door all the way for the grinning fool.

"I had you, didn't I?"

"Not really." I shrugged and turned my back to him before smiling. "I knew you'd pull a prank like that." Actually, I was surprised he didn't have Jake at the door while he stood off to the side. Just to make it even funnier.

"Sure you did." Corbin knew he had gotten to me.

Drats, that man!

Once we were seated, I looked around the restaurant. He had chosen a new Italian place on the outside of the shopping mall where I had my mishap. Would I ever *not* be reminded of that day?

I could see it now. I'd be eighty-eight years old and living in a retirement home. Corbin and I would be sitting at a table playing cards, and he'd bring it up out of the blue and laugh. But it wouldn't be the same laugh he had today—it'd be more of a cackle. The kind where he'd lose his false teeth. That would make me laugh. At him.

"So, last night. It went really well. I didn't have a single mishap." I was quite proud of myself for making it through a very long day of food, drinks, and even fireworks without a single incident.

Maybe I just needed to stay away from the Christmas Crazy and I'd do fine.

Corbin kept his eyes on his menu and nodded. "Have you decided what you want yet?"

He was hiding something.

I put my menu down and glared at him. "Alright, out with it. What's going on?"

I watched as he nervously folded his arms in front of him and then unfolded them.

As he squirmed, I sat there watching, not saying a thing.

"Why don't we just enjoy the dinner and we can talk about this later?" He still wouldn't look me in the eye.

"Corbin, neither of us will be able to enjoy the night now that there's something hanging over us. You better come clean." I wasn't sure what I'd do if he didn't, but there was no way my stomach would be able to enjoy dinner knowing that something bad was coming. "Besides, it's always better to get the bad news out of the way so you can then share the good news."

"Right, like a band-aid." He blew out a breath. "Alright, because everyone was talking about us being a cute couple, our parents all think we should attend more events this season, together."

I waited, but didn't hear anything bad coming out. Except... "Wait, are you saying this isn't a real date? This is more of a business arrangement?"

Ouch, that hurt. I sat back hard in my chair and glared at him. When he'd called and said it was a date, he should have been honest about it all. I would have been fine with doing something to help my reputation as long as I knew the situation up front. Instead, he had gotten my hopes up.

Corbin's hands went up, then he quietly proceeded to explain the situation. "It's not like that. Tonight is a date. I want this." He motioned between us. "This isn't a society event—it's just you and me, together. Which is what I wanted. But our parents think it would be good for us both to be seen together as a couple at the seasonal events this month." When he paused, he looked at me knowingly.

Oh, no. He wasn't suggesting what I was thinking he was suggesting. Was he?

I held up a hand. "Are you saying I need to attend the Christmas Crazy parties this month?"

A weak smile spread across his features, and Corbin nodded. "Yeah, I am. But look at it this way, I'd be with you. And I can help make sure nothing goes wrong. A few of these parties should be exactly what the doctor ordered."

I put my head in my hands. "Why is this happening to me? I'm a good person, aren't it?" I looked up to see Corbin's sad gaze on me.

"Honestly, I don't think it's all your bad luck. I think some of it has been jealous people playing bad pranks on you."

I snorted. "You think someone intentionally pushed me in the mud outside that store last month?"

He sat there contemplating my question for a moment, then shook his head. "No, that could have happened to anyone. But all of your mishaps in high school, they started out as jealous girls messing with you."

It made no sense. I'd had bad luck my entire adult life. "What about all the issues I've had as an adult? Besides the Christmas Crazy ladies at that dress shop."

"I've actually thought about this a lot over the past few days, and more after the sermon today. Did you pick up on the concept of negative thinking?" Corbin paused and waited for me to answer.

I thought about it for a moment. "Yeah, I thought about that earlier. Negative thinking has a power all its own. And positive thinking does as well. What we think long term tends to shape who we are, and what happens to us." I had wondered about that today. Could I have let those sour girls in high school develop my self-worth in a way that led to my incidents?

"For as long as I can remember, girls have been jealous of our friendship. And the more popular ones tended to tease you a lot. Some even pulled mean pranks on you. Do you think your self-confidence took such a beating for so long that when you left, things continued to happen?" He hadn't gone to college with me, but he probably did keep up on what had happened in my life.

But to be honest, once I left town for college, life got infinitely better for me. The incidents did taper off. My freshman year of college was tough, but my roommates really helped me. In fact, they became such great friends that we still kept in touch, even though we all lived in different parts of the country.

With that thought in mind, I went through my memories of life since becoming an adult, and it was very possible there was something to what Corbin had said, as well as what the pastor had said. There was power behind negative and positive thinking.

We are who we think we are.

Could it be that simple? Forget about falling out of that stupid dress shop, it really could have happened to anyone. But most of what had happened to me over the years could have been avoided. Even the cake on the seat could have been avoided if I hadn't felt the need to sit down because I was such a klutz.

Were my negative thoughts toward myself causing me to make bad decisions that led to stupid incidents?

"Okay, I can see that, somewhat. But what about you throwing the football at me? That wasn't something I could have avoided."

"But maybe you could have avoided it. Or *we* could have avoided it. Both of us saw you in one light. Then that night you changed everything, and I was in shock. And I'll bet the only reason you fell into the pool was because of the heels you had on. You didn't normally wear high heels. You must have lost your balance and then stumbled around until you fell in."

Corbin made some good points.

But could it be that simple? I let some stupid, slutty girls affect my own self-worth so much that I tanked myself? Or put myself in situations that ended badly? Could it really be that simple? "I don't know. I suppose it's possible. I'll have to think on it some more."

The more I thought about it, the more it all sounded right. As time had gone on, away from Corona, I did end up feeling better about myself and the frequency of incidents had gone way down.

Chapter 23

Corbin

D inner with Millie the previous night was eye-opening for us both. And it wasn't about our relationship this time. Thanks to services on Sunday, and God's influence, we learned a lot about how much our minds can control us.

They really are a lot like computers.

"Bella!" I called out for my dog so we could go for a walk down to the local coffee shop. Not only do they love it when I bring in Bella, but they also sell doggy treats in addition to the best coffee concoctions around. And I was going to need more caffeine, and a good walk, if I was going to clear my head and get ready for a late-night Zoom meeting with my Taiwanese client.

I chuckled when Bella brought me her leash. "I see you read my mind?"

Speaking of my mind...I got back to thinking about the topics from yesterday as I took my Bella out for an evening stroll.

It's so important to input the right data in order to get a positive output. If you input bad data, the output is going to be all wrong. Just like in life. It's amazing how much I still had to learn about life and the human body. How many people understood the need for positive thinking?

Sure, psychopaths understand that in order to get their prey where they want them, they have to inundate the person, or people, with negative thoughts. But I had never realized it worked with regular people, too. And the power of positive thinking is so much more important.

No wonder the self-help gurus were making so much money. People were getting what they needed to succeed. Sadly, some of those authors and speakers weren't good people, but the messages were the important thing. In order to succeed in anything, you had to believe in yourself. And not listen to the negativity around you, or more importantly, the negative thoughts that could sometimes inundate your mind when you least expected it.

Not only do human enemies use negativity to attack us, but so does the devil. Thinking back to some key moments in my life, unexpected negative thoughts entered my mind all on their own. Thoughts I would have never conjured on my own. Thoughts meant to harm me, not help me.

But God says he wants to prosper us, not harm us. What was that Bible verse? Something from Jeremiah, but I wasn't sure what it was. So I did a quick internet search on, "plans to prosper you."

What came up was Jeremiah 29:11 – *For I know the thoughts that I think toward you, saith the Lord, thoughts of peace, and not of evil, to give you an expected end.* KJV

While the NIV version was a little different, it still said that God wants us to have peace, and to prosper us.

Basically, what I discovered is that God thinks positive thoughts for us. And since I know that the devil is contrary to God, he most likely thinks negative thoughts for us, and against us.

The Bible is full of scripture that states God loves us. I think that if I ignored the negative thoughts and actively thought positive ones, then life would be much better. It would certainly be different.

And that was exactly what Millie needed, too. She was a beautiful, caring person. And I wasn't just thinking about how she looked on the outside. She'd spent so much of her life helping others, and not just with the orphanage in Africa. I knew she also helped locally.

It was sad that based on her bad experiences in high school she had such low self-esteem. She was so much better than she believed. But maybe, just maybe, after the lessons this week she'd come to realize how much she really did have to give the world, and how wonderful she was.

If Millie and others who suffer from low self-esteem could start thinking positively about themselves, then maybe they could change the negativity in their own lives. This was something I wanted to help her with. Even if we never got past a few dates, and our relationship only stayed as friends, I'd do whatever it took to help her.

Too many women and men today have issues with their own self-worth. It's time we all started to think positively and ignore the negative thoughts and statements about ourselves. I hoped I wasn't one of those people who threw out negativity like it was going out of style. I wanted to be known as a positive person.

From here on out, I was going to be positive and not share in gossiping. Even if what went around was true, it wasn't an uplifting thing to spread rumors about someone else's life. Gossip was one of those things that also contributed to low self-esteem.

So with that thought in mind, I called up Millie. "Hey, beautiful."

I could hear her sigh on the other end and I wasn't sure if it was one of those kind that women did when they were happy, or when they were sad. "Is everything all right?"

"It is now. How are you doing today?" Her response wasn't exactly chipper, but it wasn't fatalistic, either.

"I'm great now that I'm on the phone with you."

I heard her chuckle on the other end and knew that she was relaxing, like I was. Talking to her lately was becoming easier and easier, like when we were kids and best friends.

"I take it you're calling me about the party this Saturday?"

She'd remembered my work party. That sent a thrill of excitement through my bones. And the fact that she didn't sound upset was even better. "Yeah, I wanted to make sure you were still good to go and set the time to pick you up."

We spoke for a few minutes about the party and the dress. Since it was a company Christmas party for one of my biggest clients, we'd be expected to dress up, just like any other Christmas party we'd attended during Decembers of the past.

"I have a few dresses I can choose from, especially since none of those attending this party will have seen me at past parties." Millie was one of those who ascribed to the philosophy that you couldn't wear a formal, or even semi-formal, dress more than once if the same people were going to see it.

Me? I thought that was crazy. I had a few nicer suits and I just switched out them out depending on my mood. Although, I could change up the shirt and tie I wore, so it was a bit different than a dress. I didn't think women could do anything to make a dress look a little different.

"So, what had you sounding so sad when I called?" I still knew her well enough to know when she didn't sound like her normal, chipper self.

She paused for a moment and then started telling me about her day. Apparently she ran into Melinda. Of all the people for her to see when she was working on her self-esteem.

"Millie, you do know that Melinda says what she does because she's jealous of you, right?"

"What, me? How can that be true?"

In high school Melinda hated Millie because we were best friends. Today it was probably something similar, but I'd bet it had more to do with the fact that Melinda's life was a train wreck. "Millie, you've got your career in order. You have a wonderful family and friends who adore you."

She continued my thought by saying, "And Melinda's life is an absolute wreck right now. By her own doing, but it's still got to be tough going through a divorce." Millie sighed.

She really was a nice person. Not just someone who paid lip service, either. If I knew my friend—girlfriend? Was she my girlfriend now? Was that what I wanted? Either way, Millie would probably try to do something nice for Melinda, no matter if she deserved it or not.

"You know, I've been praying for her this week. She's still married and has two kids. It would be great if she could keep her family together. They'll need a lot of counseling, but their marriage could be stronger for it if they tried."

"And if they brought God into it, right?" I'd seen a few marriages break apart over the years, and a few that struggled. Those who made it did so with God on their side.

"Very true. But hey, let's not discuss something so sad. I'm actually looking forward to seeing you on Saturday night."

Her admission had me a little bit shaken. Millie was looking forward to attending a Christmas party? "You know, if you wanted we could meet up for coffee one afternoon this week."

"Oh? How about now? I just got home from work." She sounded a bit tentative, as though this was her first time asking someone out for coffee.

"Millie, I'd really like that." Even though she couldn't see me, a smile was spreading across my face. "I'm actually on my way to the coffee shop next to the cinemas by my house."

"Is Bella with you?" She asked.

"Of course. I never take a walk without her." I chuckled and looked down when Bella looked up at me with her big, round eyes. Then she chuffed, almost as though she was inviting Millie to join us.

"See you in about fifteen minutes?"

I hung up after confirming and leaned down to pat Bella's head. "That's a good girl. I'm sure it was your company she wanted to see the most. But I'll take second place to you any day of the week." Bella licked my face and we headed toward my first coffee date with Millie.

We were actually doing this. Millie and I were meeting up for dates and I was taking her to a company Christmas party in July. She even sounded happy to be attending the party with me.

What a change from the grinch she'd been only a few short weeks earlier.

Chapter 24

Millie

Oh my gosh, oh my gosh, oh my gosh! I was really doing this. I mean, I know I had already been on a sorta date with Corbin, but this seemed different. Like a real date. Even though it was last minute and just coffee. Last night's dinner was a last-minute decision as well. But it didn't have the same heft to it.

It was almost like Corbin felt he had to take me out last night since I had no food in the house and I sounded so harried over the phone. But tonight, it was him who brought it up first. Right? I mean, I didn't just ask him out, did I? Oh! I did. Where in the world did I get the gumption to do that?

With no time to really think about what I'd just done, I changed out of my work clothes and put on a pair of tan capri's and a Hawaiian print shirt that was sure to wow Corbin. It had little islands dotting the blue background. And on those islands were a pair of lounge chairs under a palm tree. It was a truly serene display.

I hoped the shirt would give me confidence as well as tranquility. This was a big step for me. One I knew I was ready for. All day long I had thought about our conversation the night before as well as what the pastor said. I kept positive thoughts all day long. Any time someone tried to say something negative, I turned it around it my head and made it positive. Sometimes it was a challenge, but I loved a good challenge.

See, I did it right there, too.

I was getting the hang of this.

Too bad I jinxed myself.

Running a few minutes late, I parked my car as close to the coffee shop as possible and jogged to the corner that held the coffee shop. I would have noticed Corbin anywhere, especially when he was wearing one of his Santa-themed Hawaiian print shirts. Not too many people had them, let alone wore them out in public. But Corbin was confident that way. In fact, he had a healthy sense of self-esteem. I could really learn a lot from him.

I stopped short when I saw who he was talking to. It couldn't be. He wouldn't do this to me, would he? Was it all a lie? No, I wasn't going to think that way. I wasn't. Think positive. She just happened to be here, that's all.

Corbin was talking to the bane of my existence, Melinda Smith. I looked around to see if anyone else I knew was around but couldn't see anyone. There were people there, but none I knew.

Slowly, I crept closer. Doing my best to stay positive. I couldn't let this situation bring me down. Just because they were talking didn't mean a single thing. Right?

But it did.

Either I was in a nightmare, or I was suffering a heart attack right then and there. For my heart stopped beating the moment Melinda leaned in kissed Corbin right on the mouth.

Not wanting to stay and see any more of this, I turned to run away and of course what do you think happened? I ran right into a woman carrying a tray of four Frappuccino's.

They spilled all over me. And I mean *all* over. "Ah!" I looked down as chocolate flavored frozen coffee ran down the front of my shirt, on to my capri's and dotted the ground at my feet. "Great, just what I needed."

"Millie?" His voice called out to me.

But I ignored him.

Not only did I just see Corbin cheating on me with Melinda of all people, but he saw me having another embarrassing incident. Could I not get a break?

I ran away as the lady with the drinks apologized to me. Really, I should have apologized to her, since I was the one who abruptly turned tail and ran straight into her. But I didn't have time. Corbin was too close for comfort.

"Not again." I moaned as I got into my car and felt the frappe coat my seat. I was never going to get away from the negative life. And now I was going to have to pay for my car to get detailed...again.

Chapter 25

Corbin

Great, Melinda was here. That was the last thing I needed. And the last thing that Millie needed. The annoying woman must have a tracker on me, or Millie, for she always shows up at the wrong time. But to be fair, there's never a good time for Melinda to show up, anywhere.

I know that Millie thinks we should pray for her. But come on. How many times does she have to ruin an event for us? Would praying for her really help?

A long red fingernail inched its way up the front of my shirt. "Come on, Melinda. Don't do that." Would she ever get a clue?

She purred, "Oh, but Corbin, I know you want me. You've wanted me since high school. If it wasn't for that stupid oath you all took, you and I would have made the perfect couple. We'd probably still be together, too."

No, we wouldn't. However, I wasn't cruel. "Melinda, I'm with Millie now. So I'd appreciate it if you stopped trying to come on to me." I shook my head. "I'm not interested." I wanted to add – *never was and never would be*. But that would be harsh. And besides, the worst thing you could do was poke the lioness when she was down. Or was it poke the bear? Either way, attacking her when she was already injured from the whole councilman debacle wasn't going to help the situation.

Melinda tilted her head and grinned like the she-devil she was. I swear, I had no idea what was coming. If I did, I would have backed up so far, I'd be on the moon. Instead, I tried not to cause a scene, and ended up making one of the biggest mistakes, ever. Ever worse than the football in high school.

The clammy lips that hit mine caused my stomach to roil. If I wasn't so shocked, I would have pushed her away from me so hard, she would have fallen. Instead, I took a moment to clear my head from the disgusting display happening to me and calmed down. Once I knew I wasn't going to hurt the woman, I took her by her arms and pulled myself away from her.

It was all I could do to keep the anger from bursting forth.

The evil creature that she was, she actually tried to get closer to me. "Come on, baby, I know you want this."

I growled out in a low voice so as not to bring too much attention, "no, I don't." I took three steps back and held my hand up in front of us. "Look, Melinda, we've known each other since high school so I don't want to hurt you, but I've never been interested in you. Not ever. The word *no* should go both ways. So I'm saying no. Stop it. And don't ever touch me again. You're a married woman with kids. I think it's high time you remembered that."

I didn't even wait for a reply. I knew she'd have a slick come back but I wasn't buying anything that came out of her mouth. The woman had a forked tongue that was as smooth as silk.

When I turned around, I was horrified.

"Millie?" I gasped and started before taking off in her direction. She had seen Melinda kissing me. I knew exactly what she'd think. And was that a Frappuccino all over her? "Not again."

It was only yesterday that she started to think positive. With this debacle, I could only pray it wouldn't take another fourteen years to get her to speak to me again. I moved toward Millie but had a head start and was running. I'd never make it to her before she got into her car and sped away.

Would she answer my call? I had to try. So I pulled out my phone and dialed. It went to voicemail. If she was going to screen my calls, I'd just have to go to her house.

Thirty minutes later, I was sitting on the steps to her front porch. I knew she was inside because her car was there, but she refused to answer the door or her phone. I couldn't hear anything inside, but since her car was there, she must have been as well.

I just had to get Millie to listen to me. What happened wasn't my fault, honestly. If I had suspected what Melinda had in store, I'd have moved far away from her. How in the world could that demon think kissing me in public would be a good idea? Did she see Millie walking up?

I thought back to the timing of it all and cringed when I remembered her cold, clammy lips on mine. Just before she went in for the kiss, she did seem to look over my shoulder and the expression on her face...

Oh, she was even more calculating than I'd ever given her credit for. How could I not see how she was manipulating the situation? What was I going to do now? Would getting a boombox and standing in a raincoat out front of Millie's house playing "In Your Eyes" by Peter

Gabriel work? I doubted it. But, if there was any chance at it's success, I'd do it.

Jeannie, she'd know exactly what to do. I should have gone to Millie's best friend back in high school but every time I got near her, she sneered and ran away. Just like Millie.

But not this time.

This time I wasn't taking no for an answer. Which was odd since I just gave Melinda that speech about hearing me say no. However, this was different. I needed Millie to know the truth.

Chapter 26

Millie

*H*ow could he? I was so embarrassed, and it was all my fault. Of course, he would be interested in Melinda. She was beautiful and popular, even with this scandal surrounding her. But why would Corbin take me out and spend so much time with me if he was interested in someone else?

Was it all because of our mom's?

Did he do this just to appease them?

No, it couldn't be that. Could it? I was so confused.

The moment I entered my house I ran to the bathroom and showered. Where of course I was reminded of the incident from last month. At least this time I stayed on my feet. That was something, right?

Maybe there was something to this positive thinking thing? As I sat on the edge of my sunken tub I put my head in my hands and cried. I hated crying, it always left me with a headache and a puffy face. Not just red eyes.

I was doomed to always get hurt, wasn't I? Especially when it came to Corbin. Who, kept trying to call me. I'd even bet he was the one knocking on my door and ringing the doorbell. Thankfully, he gave up and left. I wasn't going to deal with him, not now.

Especially not when I was covered in a cold, coffee concoction.

Correction, four cold coffee concoctions.

Instead, once I finished crying, I got into the tub where I proceeded to soak in a long, hot bath with my latest bath bomb, a silky-sweet Caribbean flowery scent. Instead of depending on Calgon to take me away, I was being cleaned and lulled by the Caribbean Lily.

As I cleaned up I thought about what I was going to do. I couldn't keep living like this. Being so negative and letting everything affect me so badly, that I tripped up and caused accidents, was no way to live.

When I was in Maine, life wasn't this difficult.

I had to remind myself that I was a strong, independent woman and I didn't *need* a man to make me whole. Only God could do that.

But I wanted Corbin.

I always had.

Ugh! Would I ever get past him? Maybe if I moved away?

No, that was falling into my old patterns. And just last night I promised God during my nightly prayer I wouldn't fall back into that old pattern.

No running away this time. Instead, I'd accept that Corbin just isn't that into me and I'd move on. Maybe this was just what I needed to get him out of my system for good?

Yes, that was it. I was going to do a Corbin-cleanse. Just how exactly that worked, I wasn't sure, yet. Maybe Jeanie would know? Of course, she would. My best friend always had the answer when I needed it.

Tomorrow I'd call her and find out what I should do. Then I'd be able to get past my infatuation for Corbin. That was all it was. An unrequited infatuation that had gone all the way back to high school. If I could *finally* get over him, I just knew that everything would be so much easier.

But tonight? Tonight, I would get comfy and sit on the couch watching Jane Austen movies and eating ice cream. Yes, that was it. I was going to give myself one night to wallow in my misery, then tomorrow I'd put on my big girl panties and move forward.

And the best part? I didn't have to do any of those stupid Christmas Crazy in July events that my mom wanted me to attend. Oh, bonus! I wasn't going to hide out under a rock, but I also wasn't going to be all Christmas Crazy, either. No, I'd work and be the best darned employee my company had seen since the pandemic started. Then, I'd sit at home on July twenty-fifth watching my Start Trek marathon and eating popcorn.

There, that would teach those crazy people not to mess with Christmas!

Well, okay, to be fair, I doubted anyone other than my own family would even notice I'd gone on a Christmas strike. But, if anyone else noticed, I'd tell them that Christmas was in December, not July. "Hmph."

Turned out, it wasn't as easy as I thought it would be. The next evening when I called Jeanie, she took *his* side. I mean, come on!

"Jeanie, how in the world can you believe his assertions that he didn't kiss her? I saw it with my own two eyes!" I yelled through the phone. She was crazy to believe him.

"Millie, he's so upset. And angry."

"Angry? What does *he* have to be angry about? *I'm the one* he was supposed to be meeting for coffee last night! And she was the one he was kissing! Argh!" I paced my living room, not even believing what I was hearing from my best friend. It would have made sense if I was talking to Jake. Of course he'd believe whatever dribble Corbin had come up with. But Jeanie? How could she?

"He's angry because she assaulted him." Jeanie sighed and I could imagine her running a hand over her face and she tried to tell me what she was thinking. "I think you need to talk to him. Let him tell you his side of the story. He really was there to meet you, not her. She Shanghaied him. He was so shocked, he froze. Then by the time he extricated himself from her claws, you were already turned around."

"No, no." I shook my head, not believe it. "How could Melinda have kissed him without him stopping her? It makes no sense."

"Did you see his arms around her? Did it look like he was enjoying it?"

I thought back to what I had seen and shivered. The image would forever be seared in my mind. But, when I evaluated the memory, I did notice that Corbin's arms were down at his side. Could it be? No. "Even if she did surprise him, he could have easily pulled back, or better yet, moved his head so she couldn't have kissed him. Why was she even so close to him to begin with?"

"You know how sneaky and conniving she is. Think about, Millie. I mean really think about it. Didn't you tell me that Corbin told you he wanted to date you?"

"That was just to keep the heat off of me. It was a ruse set up by my mom and his mom. That was all it was." That much I was sure of.

"Millie, when are you going to get it through that thick skull of yours that he's into you? And why would he invite you to coffee if he was meeting Melinda?" Jeanie's tone indicated she had hit the nail on the head with her observation, but I knew better.

"Melinda probably did surprise him. He was probably meeting me for coffee to let me down nicely. I bet he was planning on telling me all about her last night." Although, something in the back of my mind was starting to niggle.

Corbin had already been walking to the coffee shop with Bella when we spoke on the phone. And if memory served, it really was me who suggested we meet up for coffee. So, it couldn't have been planned. However, if he had already spoken to Melinda and told her he was walking Bella to the coffee shop, maybe she planned on meeting him there to surprise him? If they were starting to see each other, that would be plausible.

But the whole divorce and councilman thing? Would Corbin really attach himself to a woman going through that much drama? He wouldn't? Would he?

"Just talk to him. Hear him out. That's all I ask." Jeanie pleaded over the phone.

"Why are you taking his side? Why do you want me to talk to him so badly?" Jeanie had never taken his side before. Okay, so maybe she had told me after college that I should try and patch things up with Corbin, but she wasn't this demanding then, why now?

Jeanie sighed. "I'm not taking his side. I'm always on your side, Millie. But I do think you might not have seen the whole thing as it really went down. Or you misinterpreted it. I think you need to let him tell you his side. There's always two sides to a story."

"I'll think about it." And I would, after I prayed about it. I'd need a huge dose of wisdom from God if I was going to look more into this.

"That's all I can ask." Jeanie hung up, promising to talk to me again soon.

I sat there on my couch looking at nothing in particular and wondering if she was right. Did I misinterpret the situation?

Melinda was definitely devious enough to pull off something like that. But, was Corbin really as innocent as Jeanie made him out to be?

Chapter 27

Corbin

I t had been two days since I'd spoken to Jeanie. Two horrific days of waiting to see what Millie would do. Jeanie said to wait and let Millie call me when she was ready. I had promised I would, but I couldn't.

Yesterday, I texted her. No response.

Today, I sent her an email. Still no response.

I had to do something drastic. Something that would get her attention and show her how much I cared.

That scene from *Say Anything* kept repeating in my head over and over. I wasn't really the romantic sort. You could ask any of my ex-girlfriends. I was more the action sort. But, I did know enough to know it was going to take something over the top to get Millie's attention.

For about two seconds I considered calling Jake, but he wasn't romantic, either. The man had only had one girlfriend for more than a month, how would he know what to do?

I sat there, laughing at what Jake might consider doing to get a woman's attention and shook my head. "Bella, how would you like for a male dog to get your attention?" I thought about what I just said and shook my head when my little dog tilted her head and looked at me as though I was an idiot.

"You're right. A human woman wouldn't want me sniffing around her backside. Okay, so you won't be any help." I patted Bella's head and she gave me light chuff, sounding as though she agreed with my statement.

Then, my phone rang and my heart soared. Thinking it was Millie I almost stumbled over my own feet as I scrambled to get to my phone and answer it before it went to voicemail. So when I missed the name on caller ID I was shocked to hear a male voice greeting me.

"So, I hear you're no better at getting a woman to give you a second chance than I am." Jake joked, and I sank on the chair.

"Hey, Jake. How'd you hear?" Of course, he'd already know about my Millie issues. Someone was probably watching everything go down at the shopping center Monday night.

"I have my spies." Jake chuckled.

"Who else saw what happened? And what social media..." I stopped midway when an idea hit me. "Jake, I gotta go! I just came up with a brilliant plan to get Millie back. Keep an eye on my social media channels and be sure to like and share what I post this afternoon." I hung up before he could even respond.

I had it. I knew I did. Now, to just get the right tools to make it work. I was about to give the gossip mill something to really talk about.

It took all night to get it right, but the moment I posted on TikTok, I knew it was the way to go. When I woke up later this morning, I was shocked, and excited, to see how many views, likes, comments, and shares my little video had received. Using the proper hashtags really helped my video. It looked as though it was on its way to going viral, just what I needed.

While there weren't any messages from Millie, yet; there were a ton from other friends. Jake had already tried to call me three times and sent five messages. I'd better call him first.

Laughing, I made my way to the coffee maker and dialed my best friend.

"Corbin, it's about time. Where have you been? Please tell me that you've spent all morning talking to Millie and patching things up?" The excitement in Jake's voice told me he'd seen the video. Even if his messages hadn't told me what he thought, I'd still know why he was so excited.

"Whoa, calm down. First, tell me what's been going on. I just woke up." I rubbed the sleep from my eyes and waited as my friend began to tell me what he had seen, and heard.

It only took a minute before my single-cup coffee was done. And I was sipping away while listening to Jake go on and on about the latest social media craze.

"Most everyone is very positive. There are a few negative Nelly's, but overall everyone loves what you've done. Shoot, I love it. Do you mind if I steal this idea?" Jake laughed.

It was good to hear him laugh and sound happy. Since Sonya broke his heart, he hadn't been the same. Now, however, he was back to his normal carefree self. Well, except for wanting to do something romantic for a woman. That was new.

"As long as you promise not to do it to get Sonya back, sure. Wait, you can only use my move if the woman passes muster. I first must approve of her." Most of the women Jake went out wouldn't pass muster, they weren't intended to be long-term girlfriends, so he only went for beauty, not brains.

If my best buddy wanted a real girlfriend, she needed to be nice and intelligent, in addition to any outside beauty she might possess.

"Oh, no. I'm not ever going back to Sonya. No worries there. You were right about her. She's only interested in money and prestige. No thank you."

I could picture Jake shaking his head vehemently as he stated he was never letting that viper back in his life again.

"Good, glad to hear it. But, buddy, is there someone else you want to get back?" My video really was more for getting a girl back, or at least getting her attention. But, if it was for a stranger, she'd surely think the man doing it was a psycho stalker.

"Nah, not yet. But down the road, there might be. One never knows when they'll finally grow up and want a real relationship. And when that time comes, I'm sure I'll do something to mess it up. And I'll need a grand gesture in my back pocket."

"Ah, yes. The grand gesture. Well, what I did will only work if the lady in question knows anything about pop culture, or eighties movies." I laughed thinking about how Millie had gotten me to watch *Say Anything*, once. I actually think I liked it more than she did. That woman really did like it when things were blown up, or cars crashed.

Thankfully, when she was in the mood for chick flicks, she called up Jeanie and they'd watch them together.

I still remembered how we'd watch Star Trek Enterprise together over the phone when we were kids. That was before we had our own cell phones, and we'd tie up the landlines for more than an hour because, you know, we had to discuss the show when it was over. Commercial breaks were for getting up to get snacks or drinks, or answer our parents' questions. Then, when the show was over, we'd spend another hour dissecting the show and speculating about what would happen next.

Right then and there, a pang hit my heart so horribly, that I wondered if I was having a heart attack. I really missed those simpler days. "Do you think Millie will see it and agree to hear me out?"

There was a slight pause and I wondered if I dropped the call somehow.

"Yes, I think she will see it and call you up. Maybe not right away, but she will call. Hang in there." All joking had left his Jake's voice and he was being serious for a change.

"Thanks, Man." I really did appreciate his insight. Even though his track record was so much worse than mine, it was still nice to hear he thought it would work.

Some days, I absolutely love working from home. Then others, like today, I hated it. The hours dragged by as I waited to hear from Millie. How could she not have seen it yet? Someone else would have even if she was on a social media hiatus. Which I would normally wholeheartedly support.

Just not today.

No, today Millie Milan just *had* to look at her social media, even just one account. Someone in her list of contacts would have tagged her at the very least.

Just then, Bella, my ever-faithful companion, sat at my feet holding her leash in her mouth.

I couldn't help but smile when she showed up right when I needed her. "Alright, Girl. Let's go for a walk. That should help us both out." After I clasped the leash to her collar, I rubbed behind her ears and we took off for a walk.

I prayed that God would give me patience, and that Millie would see the posting, somehow, someway.

And then she'd call.

Chapter 28

Millie

E ven though my boss specifically called me last week and said he wanted me in the office going forward, I had tried to get him to allow me to work from home for a couple of days.

The Grinch said no.

Of course, he did. I was in the negative mood, again. Everything seemed to be going wrong for me.

Yesterday, Simone Craven walked into me while I was standing in the breakroom. Standing, mind you! And of course her fresh mug of coffee spilled all over the front of my newer suit. Since I was the unlucky one, Simone had zero splashes of mostly creamer coffee on her exquisite dress. That right there sent me into a downward spiral.

I had stopped calling it bad luck, it was now known as negative luck. Would I ever get back into the positive zone?

Thankfully, today was Thursday. And Friday's we all worked from home, so it was my last day in the office for this week. After yesterday's fiasco, I had decided to stick to my cubicle unless I was about to pee my pants. Then I could get up and use the facilities and top off my coffee or water. Otherwise, I was glued to my chair.

That would make it more difficult for anything negative to happen. But by doing so, I also missed out on the water-cooler talk, or gossip as some called it.

I did hear a few snippets about some new TikTok video making the rounds. Those were either good, or bad. Maybe when I needed a break from the editing I was working on I'd get on my phone and see what the hullabaloo was all about. But for now, my phone was off and I had no desire to turn it on, yet.

"Millie, you're so lucky." Anna said as she walked past my cube.

When I looked up, she was sighing and slowly heading toward her desk. She had just come from the breakroom. But why was I lucky?

I looked around the room and noticed a few people smiling in my direction. Lance gave me two thumbs up, while Gretchen winked at me.

Something weird was going on.

I lowered my head and ignored everyone, almost afraid to find out what the deal was. Since I now was back in the negative zone, something bad must have happened. But if that was the case, then why were so many people smiling at me? Why did Anna think I was lucky?

Decisions, decisions...

But I only held out for a few seconds before I grabbed my purse out of the drawer and rifled through it looking for my phone.

When I turned it on, there were over one hundred notifications. "What?" I blinked a few times and refreshed my screen. Yup, I had been inundated with messages from too many people to name. All coming from various social media apps. Then there were five missed calls, mostly my mom. But one was Jeanie. And my best friend had also texted me almost a dozen times.

Shoot, it wasn't even two in the afternoon yet. What had happened?

Worried that something happened to one of my family members, I called Jeanie first.

"It's about time you call me!" Exasperation laced her words. Then excitement filled the static over the line. "Did you see it? What'd you think?"

"See what? What's going on, Jeanie?"

"What, are you living under a rock?" My friend laughed into the phone. "The TikTok from Corbin, of course. It's gone viral."

"Uh, no. My phone's been off all day. Give me a sec and I'll pull up my account." I left her on the line because I knew she'd flip out if I hung up. She would want to be the first person I spoke to after seeing whatever was going on. And I didn't want to disappoint her.

With all of the notifications I had from the app in question, it was very easy to find the original posting.

At first, I didn't know what I was watching. It was Corbin, but he held what I took to be a boombox from the eighties. And it was large. It reminded me of a scene from an old movie, but I couldn't remember. Corbin held the boombox in front of his face and I saw the top of his head over the top of the old-style music player, bobbing up and down.

"What?" Oh, that's right. I had my sound off. Clicking the button on the side of my phone, I sat back in my chair when the music started as I replayed the video. "Oh, is that?" No, it couldn't be.

But it was.

Corbin played the song from the movie Say Anything. You know, the one from Peter Gabriel. He had reenacted that scene where John Cusack was trying to win back Ione Skye's love.

Wait, what? At the end of the video he did, there was a caption, "*Millie, Please let me explain. It's not what you think.*"

I put my phone up to my ear. "Jeanie, was that for me? Really?"

"Yes, sweetie, it is." Jeanie paused a moment, then said, "Will you call him?"

I had to. Didn't I? How could I not after he'd done what he did for me? I looked back at the screen and seen that over one million views had been logged along with almost one hundred thousand shares. "Wow, yeah. I guess so. What does this mean?"

"It means, silly, that you got it wrong. He really does care for you. No man would do something like that for just anyone." I could hear the exasperation from her coming over the line, and I smiled.

"Really? You think Melinda surprised him with that kiss? That he wasn't into it?" I had wondered over the past two days if I had gotten it wrong. I *prayed* I had gotten it wrong, but how could I know?

"Millie, you have to decide if you can trust Corbin, or not. If it were me, I'd trust him."

I knew she was right. My old insecurities were rearing their ugly little heads, not to mention the little devil sitting on both of my shoulders trying to tell me I'm not worthy of a man like Corbin. But, I am worthy. If I'm worthy of God's love and forgiveness, then I'm worthy of any man's love. The Bible is very clear that God loves us and forgives. Maybe I should forgive Corbin?

Wait, is there even anything to forgive?

The more I thought about it, the more I realized that if Corbin was anything like the boy I used to know, he would never choose to be with a woman like Melinda.

Not that I was judging her, because I had no idea if the Biblical values even pertained to her. If she wasn't saved, then the Bible's rules didn't apply to her. Sure, the law stated that you weren't supposed to cheat on a spouse, but no one went to jail for that anymore. And women could no longer be stoned for getting caught with a man who wasn't her husband.

But Corbin?

He was a Christian. And the rules in the Bible did apply to him. He wouldn't be with someone who cheated on her husband. No matter how beautiful she was. Nor would he willingly kiss one woman while waiting for another he had just made plans with.

Maybe Jeanie had been right all along?

Maybe Corbin was into me?

There was only one way to find out. I'd have to swallow my pride and call him. The only problem was that I didn't want to have this conversation over the phone while I was at work.

So, I did the next best thing – I liked and shared his video.

"Thanks Jeanie. I'll see if he's willing to talk tonight." Then I hung up and spent the next ten minutes trying to figure out what to say to him.

It was a good thing I was ahead in my work.

I kept going back and forth with should I call him or text him? I didn't want to get into a discussion about any of it now, but I also felt as though a text message to set up a meeting was too...casual? Unprofessional? Heartless? The word was there somewhere, and maybe it was all of those words combined.

However, I knew I couldn't call him. Not yet. He'd want to talk and I couldn't do that here. These cubical walls have ears, and they talk.

Instead, I sent this text – *Hey Lloyd. Nice TikTok. Too bad Diane didn't have TikTok back in the eighties. BTW, I love it. Can we talk tonight? IRL?*

Immediately, I received his reply asking about coming to his place straight from work. He'd have dinner ready if I could. I'd never turn down a homemade meal from Corbin.

Even after we finished our quick chat via text, I felt a little bit better. Work was still tough. But thankfully, for the drive home I was able to listen to an audiobook. Sadly, it kept reminding me of Corbin.

Chapter 29

Corbin

I t worked! It really did work.

Or at least, the video worked well enough to get Millie to talk to me. Now it was up to me to convince her that Melinda was only up to her normal tricks. I had nothing to do with it.

Well, not of my own free will I didn't. She played me as well as Millie. I'd have to forgive Melinda for her trick, but I was still too mad to think about that. Right now, I needed to plan a nice meal for tonight and figure out a way to get Millie to hear me, really hear what I had to say.

I could understand her reticence. Melinda and her cronies had done a number on Millie back in high school. And I was too stupid to really see it...or do anything about it. If only I knew then what I know now. Everything would have been very different.

Not being a chef, or even a great cook, I'd have to think hard about to make. And then I'd have to go to the store. "Bella! Let's go for a walk."

Once my trusty canine companion and I were outside, it suddenly hit me. I was overcome by the scents in the air and I knew what I was going to make. Sometimes, living close to fabulous restaurants was a good thing. Like now.

Bella and I went to the local grocery store where I was able to get all of the needed ingredients.

When the time finally arrived for Millie to show up, I kept an ear out for her knock while I fired up the grill. When we were kids, she loved anything that came off the grill. I could only hope she hadn't become one of those crazy "clean" eaters, or anything like that. But wait, she did eat barbequed meat and seafood at the picnic, so all should be fine, right?

The table was set with my only real plates. Normally, I used paper plates since it was just me. But tonight called for something nicer. So the blue and white seashell patterned plates my parents bought me when I moved into my apartment out in Orange County were what I had set. They matched well, according to my mother, with the sea blue napkins. Also purchased by her. And of course, I had to have a nice set of silverware, not the mismatched stuff I'd picked up at the dollar store while in college. So there was a shiny matching set of cutlery on the table as well.

Would it be too much to set up a candle? Probably. If this were a real date, I'd do the whole romantic vibe - lower the lights, set up some nicely scented candles that matched, and even put on soft music. But this wasn't a date. It was a chance for me to explain my side of the events that transpired the other day. And to make sure she understood that the only person I wanted to kiss was Millie Milan. No one else was even on my radar.

Before I could even put the steaks that had been marinating all afternoon on the grill, the doorbell rang. Bella barked and ran to the door, her little stub of a tail wagging as best it could. Boston Terriers didn't really have tails, it was more like a little thumb sticking out of their backside, but it did move when they were excited. Which could only mean one thing – Millie was here.

I swear, sometimes it felt like Bella liked Millie more than me.

When I stopped at the front door, my hand shook and I decided to take a moment to breath. Then I reached for the doorknob and opened the door with a smile. "Millie. I'm so glad you could make it."

For a second, I thought she might have pulled a Corbin and send Jake, or Jeanie, in her stead. But this really wasn't the time to be pulling practical jokes, even though it would have been a good way to get us both to lower our guards.

Instead, Millie stood there, looking about as nervous as I felt.

"Hey, there." Millie waved her hand and a toothless smile barely showed on her face. Then she looked down and a real smile covered her face as she bent to greet Bella.

My little dog licked Millie's face and chuffed her greeting.

"Well, hello to you, too, little Bella. I've missed you so much." Millie leaned in and gave my dog a hug. The way Bella's paws and head moved around Millie, it almost looked like she was returning the hug.

"Won't you come in? I was just about to put the steaks on the grill. You still like rib-eye steak, right?" I didn't really have anything else. It probably would have been smart of me to also make some chicken. Women appreciated a good grilled chicken breast... Right?

Millie bit her lower lip and it drew all of my attention to her mouth. All thoughts of grilling steak left me and the only thing I wanted to do was capture her lips in mine. When I felt myself moving closer to her, and my hand went out to touch her, I remembered myself and pulled back.

"Yes, I do love steak. Rib-eye is one of my favorites, right behind a bacon-wrapped Fillet Mignon."

I smiled. "Exactly. Bacon wrapped steak is one of the marvels of this world. I'll have to keep that in mind for the next time you come over for a barbecue. Come on, I have to put the steaks on, and then we can chat."

We made our way out to my tiny back patio, that really wasn't big enough for more than a grill, and a small table and chairs. The sunbrella covered most of the patio, which was great while grilling in the California sun.

"Would you like a cold glass of tea or lemonade?" I offered when I pulled out a chair for her.

After Millie took her seat, she looked up with bright eyes and nodded. "Yes, some iced tea would be wonderful. Thank you."

After the steaks had been put on the grill, and the iced tea served, I sat next to her at my small bistro table. If the evening hadn't been so hot, I would have set up the dinnerware outside so we could enjoy the fresh air while eating dinner. Maybe dessert could be served outside?

We'd have to see. That's if she stayed long enough for dessert.

Nope, I wasn't going to fall into the negative zone. I was going to be positive. Positive that all would work out as God intended, even if it wasn't what I wanted.

I've learned over the years that when my eyes, and heart, are set on God and His will, then the rest of my life works better. Sure, it sucks when things don't go the way I wanted them to, but after thirty-one years, I've seen that even when it's not what I would have chosen, if it was what God wanted then it worked out much better in the end.

That would have to go for this situation, as well. If God wanted me and Millie to *finally* be together, then it would happen. Just as long as both Millie and I were open to God's will, no she-devil could get in the way.

My nerves started to stir, and we sat there staring at our glasses. I watched as the condensation from the cold ice melted down the outside of the glass. Someone would have to start talking soon, or the night would be an unmitigated disaster.

Just as I was beginning to open my mouth, Millie spoke up, "So, it's been a few days since we spoke. How's it going?"

I had to bite my lip to keep from laughing. Benign conversation topics like the weather, or work, were exactly what I had in mind as well. "It's been good. Although, I've had a tough time concentrating this week." I wasn't about to say that all I could think about was her. No, it was too soon to put so much on her.

I stood up to flip the steaks and then looked over at her and smiled. "What about you? Have you been in the office every day so far?" I knew her boss had wanted her in the office now, and she wasn't too keen on the idea of going in every day.

Millie nodded. "Yeah, but tomorrow I get to work from home. All summer long, everyone is working from home on Fridays. Then my boss is going to re-evaluate the tele-work policy. I think they might start doing the whole *hoteling* thing."

I furrowed my brow trying to think where I'd heard that term. It sounded vaguely familiar. "Hoteling?"

Finally, she gave me a real smile. Her earlier sweet smile was for Bella, but this one was for me. Her face lit up like the sun and she even giggled. "Yup. It's where workers share office space and desks. We come in on prescribed days and setup our laptops on our desks. But days when we aren't there, another team will use those desks. It's like a hotel. You take all of your possessions with you when you leave. It's like packing for a trip. But instead of going off to some exotic location and staying at a luxurious hotel, you're just going into a smaller office."

"I see, so companies can save money on space this way." I nodded, thinking it was a good idea.

"And it helps to cut down on pollution when people don't commute as much. So the company will get credits for their employees working from home, and they get to cut their office space in half." She paused and then shrugged. "Or close to it."

"That makes a lot of sense. After the past year, so many people have learned how to work remotely, and the expenses of getting set up at home have already been incurred. It makes fiscal sense." I for one enjoyed working from home and would hate to have to go back into an office setting full time. "Although, I know from my own experience that sometimes things happen during the day and I may not spend a solid eight hours working."

"Right, but you work into the night to get your job done, right?" Millie confirmed.

I nodded. "Well, yeah. I'm my own boss. It's my company so if the work for a client isn't done, I'll lose their business."

"And if an employee doesn't get their work done on time, they could lose their job." Millie made a good point. "And with Zoom meetings, it's really easy to stay in touch with your co-workers and clients."

I could see the benefits. I didn't have to employ a dog walker since I worked from home and could walk Bella myself every day. And I did work well into the night. Even weekends one could find me behind my computer if it was needed. Since my office was set up in my home, it was very simple to get online to check something. And of course, I'd inevitably find myself working more than I planned. "I can see this working well for those who don't need to be micromanaged."

"Ugh, I hate being micromanaged. I get so much more work done on my own. Having to explain my every move to a boss is time consuming." Millie took a long drink of her tea and I sat there thinking about what she said.

I'd had micromanagers in the past. One actually wanted me to keep a daily log of every single thing I did. Which of course, took away from actual work. It was as though he didn't trust that I was doing my job. I didn't last long in that role.

When I realized we had been talking so long, I jumped up and ran to the grill. "Oh, thank goodness." I hope she liked her steak a bit more than medium. I took the rib-eyes off the grill and put them on a clean platter.

Millie picked up both of our glasses and followed me into the house where I had a tossed salad already prepared in the fridge. Then I turned on the microwave where I had two baked potatoes all seasoned, forked, and wrapped just waiting for me to turn on the timer.

The steaks needed to sit for a few minutes before we could eat them, and the salad needed to be served up, so I always waited to turn on the microwave until the moment I walked back into the kitchen.

Once everything was done, I brought the food over to the dining room table on clean serving dishes. I didn't grow up with a society mom and not learn a few things about presentation. Somehow, my mother always knew what piece of serving ware, or dinnerware, I needed. And every Christmas I always ended up with another piece to add to my collection.

I had never been more grateful for my mom than in that very moment. My table looked like something from out of a Martha Stewart photo shoot. Maybe I should have added the candles? Blue taper candles would have looked very nice. But no, that would have given off a romantic vibe, and this wasn't a romantic dinner. I needed to keep telling myself that. For if not, I'd probably reach over and grab Millie's hand and hold it. Or worse, kiss it.

Oh, drummer boy. I really needed to stop thinking about kissing Millie.

"Corbin, this steak is perfect. I love the seasonings you used. Is it a bottled rub? Or one you make yourself?" Millie cut her steak into small bite-sized pieces as she waited for my answer.

I put my knife and fork down and used the cloth napkin to wipe my mouth before speaking. "Now, that Millie, is a trade secret." I arched a brow and gave her a half-smile. "If I told you, I'd have to kill you."

Millie wiped her mouth and giggled. Her shoulders visibly relaxed and things started to feel like they had last week, or even like they did when we were young and still best friends. This was my Millie.

Yes, she was still *my* Millie. And I would do anything I could to keep her.

During dinner we talked about nothing important. We both had recently seen the latest super hero movie so we discussed it, as well as the latest Fast and the Furious movie.

"You know, we've been watching Fast and the Furious movies together since we were kids. How do these actors still look so great, and young?" I had wondered how twenty years later Michelle Rodriguez was still so hot.

"I'd actually wondered about Vin Diesel, as well. He doesn't look twenty years older, does he?" Of course, Millie would think about Vin. She'd always had a crush on him.

As we cleared away the dishes, we both recapped all of the movies and agreed we needed a Furious marathon one weekend, and soon.

"How about this weekend?" Millie asked.

And oh how I wanted to say yes. My shoulders drooped as I remembered the plans I already had for Saturday night. "I have a company Christmas in July party to attend."

"But you don't have any employees?" Millie's head tilted to the right and her perfectly manicured brows furrowed.

"Ah, but I do have clients that have large company parties. This is one I can't afford to miss." I bit my tongue before asking her to join me. We still hadn't discussed the situation, and we needed to get it all sorted before making any more plans together.

"Okay, maybe the weekend after?" The hopeful expression covering Millie's face just about melted my heart.

"What do you say we first address the elephant in the room?" I hated the way the sparkle in her eyes died when I mentioned the situation, but it had to be addressed before we moved forward. We couldn't be making plans only to have her accuse me of nonsense again. I needed her to trust me.

"Do you trust me?" That was the issue at the heart of our disagreement.

Millie sat there looking at me for a moment. "Yes, I do trust you. I guess I don't trust myself or something like that." She shrugged.

"You think your back luck, or *incidents* as you called them..."

She interrupted me. "Negative issues. I'm no longer calling them incidents or bad luck. It's all about my problem with negative thinking."

I nodded. It was a more apt description. If she focused on positivity she might not have so many problems. Well, there would still be issues. Her thinking couldn't control the world around her. But, she could control how she reacted.

"You know, if you would have just walked up to me the other day when Melinda attacked me you would have known exactly what was going on. Why didn't you?" I realized right then that her erroneous assumptions about me had hurt. I thought we had moved on and were in a good place.

But, if she didn't feel like she could walk up to me and ask about what was happening, then maybe we weren't past it all.

"When I saw Melinda..." She cleared her throat. "When Melinda attacked you, my mind went to the worst possible scenario. High school came back to me and in my stupid head that witch was telling me I was crazy to think you liked me. That you were only taking me out to these events to help my image, nothing more." She looked down at her hands holding her empty glass of tea.

Before I could answer her, I stood up and went to the counter where the pitcher of iced tea sat. I brought it back to the table and filled both of our glasses and sat back down. "So, it really wasn't about me. It was about your issues with Melinda?"

Millie nodded. "Yes, and my low self-esteem."

"But, Millie, you are such a wonderful person. Any man would be lucky to go out with you. I don't understand why you can't see that."

"I'm a work in progress. And I do think my self-worth is rising, it's just going to take a little bit of time." After she took a drink, Millie rubber her nose and I heard a little sniffle.

"I guess the question now is, do you want to date me?" I could be patient and understanding, if she was interested. "Because I do care for you and want to see where this," my hand waved between us, "goes."

"I do, too, Corbin. I'm sorry for how I treated you. I never should have doubted you. And you're right. I should have come up to you and asked what was going on. We may not have decided to be exclusive, but you were there waiting for me, not her. And even after all these years, I know you well enough to know that you wouldn't kiss one woman while waiting to meet up with another for coffee. That's not who you are."

"Thank you. I appreciate that. And just so you know, I also don't date more than one woman at a time. Even if we haven't had a discussion about exclusivity." I shook my head. There was no way I could juggle two women, or more, at a time along with owning my own company, and taking care of a dog.

The smile on Millie's face went from ear to ear. "So, that means we are exclusive?"

I chuckled. "Yes, I think we can safely say neither of us are going to date anyone else right now."

Her cheeks turned pink and my heart swelled. We were going to move forward and she was going to give me the benefit of the doubt if something like this ever happened again. Although, I'd never let Melinda get that close to me again. No hugs from her, no air kisses, nothing. I didn't even want to shake her hand. This way, there could be no more chances for her to mess things up with me and Millie.

Chapter 30

Millie

I couldn't believe Corbin and I were officially dating. Did that mean he was my boyfriend? The other night when we spoke titles weren't mentioned. Just that we were exclusively dating. Did that mean I was his girlfriend?

I was so bad at this stuff.

My feelings for the guy had changed so much these past weeks. When we first spoke after the *incident*, I almost hated him. I certainly hated myself, and that stupid mall cop. But things had begun to turn around for us both.

Now, I didn't hate anyone. Not even Melinda. And I'd heard that she had tried to get the gossip to turn on me, again. I knew she wasn't happy with how she sounded to everyone these days, but she was the one who'd made the choice to be with another man.

Even with all that, I still prayed for her. I prayed she would find her way. And I prayed that her family would get through this difficult time.

I knew that when a person was so unhappy, they could do stupid things. I'd made my share of mistakes. Hopefully, with God's help I would make better choices.

But more importantly, I started thinking positive thoughts. Even after I heard the latest attempt at changing the gossip, I didn't dwell on it. Nor, it seemed, did I have a klutzy moment, or *incident*.

Things were starting to look up for me. And as crazy as it sounded, I was looking forward to the Christmas party tonight.

Corbin and I had gone out the past two nights for coffee—decaf, of course. The best part? No Melinda sightings. But it was fun and easy. He hadn't kissed me yet, but he did come close last night.

Okay, so maybe I did have a kinda, sorta klutzy moment. The second he was moving in for the kiss, my phone went off. I was so flummoxed that I yanked back and reached for my phone. And instead of answering it, I dropped it in the grass next to where we stood in the shopping center square.

Thankfully I didn't drop it on my other side, where the water fountain was located. So, things were starting to get better. Two months ago, I would have dropped my phone in the water instead of the soft padding of the grass. So yeah, things were looking up now.

I could only pray it lasted.

By the time I was ready, I barely had enough time to get downstairs and calm my wildly beating heart. I had decided to wear a dark-green silk gown that went down to my ankles. The dress had a halter-style top. It was beaded all around the neckline and down the bodice. In the winter, I wore this dress with a black faux-mink wrap. But tonight I didn't have anything to cover my shoulders, since it was summer and so warm.

The sexy slit that went up the leg to my knee showed off the black nylons and my black high heels. I was really pushing my luck with my outfit tonight, but I felt sexy. And alive.

So alive in a way I couldn't ever remember feeling. It was no wonder my mother always said her outfits made her feel powerful. And why she always dressed so impeccably. It also helped that she had a good dose of self-esteem—something I was starting to see in myself, especially over the past two weeks. If things continued to go like this, I just might be the self-confident woman my mother had tried to teach me to be.

When the bell rang, I practically jumped. My hand flew to my heart and I had to take a deep breath. If Corbin tried to trick me tonight, I'd punch him. Not really, but I'd sure think about it. A light chuckle came out as I opened the door, ready for anything.

Except for what met me.

An exceptionally handsome man stood on my porch in a black suit with a crisp white shirt and red tie. His hair was slicked back with product, and the appreciative look he gave me told me he and I were on the same wavelength.

"Corbin, come in." I stepped out of his way and held the door for him to enter. When he walked past me, I about died and went to heaven. He smelled so good. Not only did he look like a runway model, but his scent was exactly what I imagined those models would smell like—a hint of spice with sandalwood. And if I wasn't mistaken, a tiny wisp of orange.

He was the most handsome man I'd ever met.

"Millie, you look..." Corbin took a deep breath and his eyes fluttered. "Breathtaking."

I hoped he'd picked up on the new scent I was wearing. I went to the perfume counter earlier today and picked up a new bottle of

Coco Mademoiselle Eau De Parfum. It had notes of orange, jasmine, rose, and vanilla. Not a strong vanilla, just enough to cut the stronger rose and jasmine scents down a bit. It worked so well with my body chemistry that I even attracted a few smiles from the men I passed on my way out. One even stopped me and asked what scent I was wearing.

"Thank you. You look very dashing. I think we're going to blow their socks off when we enter a room." I winked at him and was feeling a little bit cheeky tonight.

We pulled up to the Hyatt Regency Huntington Beach where the party was held, and he used the valet service. I had to admit, I was excited to be able to utilize valet service again.

The media and politicians kept talking about a "new normal." I shivered whenever they mentioned that term. It was so…unsettling. But things were pretty much normal again, almost like what they were before.

My head turned around once I was out of the car and noticed all of the expensive dresses and suits that everyone else had worn, and I was more than happy that I had chosen to wear my nicest dress. My mother could be relied upon for anything to do with fashion, and it was she who'd said I should wear this gown tonight.

While I didn't want to be the talk of the night, it was different when everyone had smiles on and commented on what a beautiful couple we made. It also helped that I didn't know any of these people. They were all strangers to me and not a single one knew about my past as the town's klutz.

It seemed anonymity really helped my confidence. Not to mention the positive thoughts I'd had all night long.

Corbin didn't stray too far from my side, and he introduced me to everyone. He didn't say if I was his date or girlfriend, but since he hadn't used the terms boyfriend or girlfriend yet when we spoke, it was probably best this way.

Mick, Corbin's client, came over to us while we were picking up hors d'oeuvres at the side table. Dinner tonight was finger food. Lots of different kinds, including these tasty crackers with some sort of schmear topped with a little shrimp. They were fabulous.

"Have you tried the bacon-wrapped cheese balls yet? They're my favorite." Mick pointed to a plate on the other end of the table that I had yet to taste.

"No, not yet. But that sounds divine." I grinned at him and Corbin.

While I wanted to go and grab one, Corbin and I had made a plan and I was sticking to it. If I wanted something, he picked it up and put it on the small plate he held. I carried several cocktail napkins and only ate one little treat at a time. So far, this plan was working, and not a single accident, or incident, had occurred. As of yet, there was nothing to be negative about, either.

Our drinks were sitting on a high-top table not too far away. Once we filled up the plate, we'd head back to the table and stand there to eat the food and take sips of our nonalcoholic drinks. We'd made the round trip twice so far, and I was hoping to make at least two more.

They had set up a sparkling cider waterfall and champagne flutes were used to drink the tasty beverages.

"Millie and I have been trying different things. So far, my favorite is the old standard of shrimp cocktail." Corbin held up one hand that had a tiny plastic cup with the red sauce in the middle and four medium shrimps hanging inside around the edges of the cup.

They were tasty, and this was our second cup to share.

"I'm so glad you were able to bring your girlfriend tonight, Corbin." Mick turned to me and continued, "I had no idea that

Corbin was seeing anyone. It's really nice to meet you. He's a great guy and an even better consultant."

I bit my lip to keep from saying I wasn't Corbin's girlfriend, but that would be rude and might embarrass Corbin. Since we hadn't had that conversation yet, I decided to just go with the flow. No need to upset the apple cart. And if I played my cards right, I just might officially be his girlfriend by the end of the night.

Corbin took a step closer to me and put one arm around my waist. He looked at me with smoldering eyes. While he responded to Mick, his full attention was on me. "It's all still so new, but I've known Millie my entire life."

"Ah, childhood sweethearts back together again?" Mick asked.

I stared directly into Corbin's sparkling green eyes and smiled. "Yes, something like that."

Corbin turned to look at Mick. "We grew up next door to each other. And we were best friends our entire childhood."

"And now you're a couple. What a wonderful story." Mick put a hand on Corbin's shoulder. "Enjoy the rest of the night. Be sure to mingle with the executive team and I'll see you both later." He turned to walk away, then looked back at Corbin. "Don't forget to pick up one of the gold bags on your way out. It's our way to say thank you for sticking with us through these last difficult months."

"Thank you, that's very generous of you." Corbin picked up one of the small plates and continued loading it up with delicious gourmet finger foods.

It was close to one in the morning when we pulled up into my driveway. Instead of turning off the engine, we sat there in a comfortable silence for a moment. I was replaying the romantic dances we'd shared earlier that evening.

When Corbin finally spoke, it was softly. "So, what did you think about what Mick said?"

"About you being a great consultant? Or the gift he gave you?" I knew what he was talking about, but I was going to tease him a little bit. Payback could be fun.

Corbin's head tilted down and he chuckled. "I meant about us being a couple."

"Oh, that comment." I didn't say anything else. Instead, I got out of the car and headed to my front porch.

Corbin followed me and when we were both standing in front of my door, he turned questioning eyes on me. "Well?"

"Well, what?" I stared back at him, trying to keep any and all emotions from showing on my face.

"You're gonna make me say it, aren't you?" One corner of his mouth tilted up. And with that one little movement, his dimple showed up and my heart melted.

"I like the idea of being your girlfriend." I gulped down my fear and asked him what he thought about being my boyfriend. Unlike the whole first date fiasco, I was going to make sure the words were used this time.

"I do, too." Then he grinned. "So, you wanna?"

I nodded. "Yeah, I do."

You know in the movies when the hero slowly goes in for a kiss and gives the lady time to say no or back away? Yeah, that didn't happen. I barely had time to say *I do* before his lips crashed into mine. It wasn't a sweet, slow kiss like in a romance book. Instead, it was raw and full of emotions that both of us had bottled up for the past fourteen years.

One of his hands was buried in my hair, while the other one held tightly to my waist. I held on to his shoulders to keep myself from falling down. The intensity, and the passion, was everything I thought a kiss with Corbin would be.

After what felt like a decade of kisses I had missed out on were finally mine, he slowed the kiss and then it became sweet and more like in the romance movies. My heart didn't even have a chance to catch up to the action, it was just getting going when he changed up the kiss again. Now, he had one of my lips between his and his arms held me firm to his body.

I put my hands on his chest and felt his heart beating in time to my own.

"I should have kissed you all those years ago." His breathless words caressed my face.

Joy infused my body and all I could do was nod. It was my fault. He had tried to make amends, but I refused to let him. I ran away just when I should have stayed put. All of those negative thoughts that had run rampant in my stupid brain, tried to come back. Especially after my latest bout with Melinda. But, I had learned too much about myself, and about how God thought about me to let the enemy win.

I wasn't going to run anymore.

Epilogue

Millie

On July twenty-fifth, Corbin and I walked into his parents' house hand in hand. Both of our families had decided to spend Christmas in July together. Now that we were all on friendly terms again, they wanted to take advantage of the opportunity.

While they all knew that Corbin and I had been spending time together and attending Christmas in July events together all month, they did not know that we were officially boyfriend and girlfriend.

That night at my door, when we decided it was what we wanted, we also decided to keep it a secret. It would be so much more fun to surprise our parents when we were all together at home. Everything else had been way too public for my liking. The gossip about the tiniest things was crazy, Christmas Crazy. So, we decided that we'd have our secret until we could speak with our parents all together.

And this little secret gave us a chance to spend Christmas Eve together watching a *Die Hard* Marathon. I had decided that a little bit of Christmas was in order. I wasn't anywhere near going Christmas Crazy, but I could enjoy the season, quietly.

And come on, who doesn't love a totally awesome, action-packed movie with a younger Bruce Willis? Also, blowing up a building on Christmas is epic!

So, when we entered the Deeks' family room where they had their family Christmas tree all set up with loads of presents beneath it, we were holding hands and smiling at each other.

I hadn't noticed, but Corbin must have, for he stopped us in the doorway and put his finger under my chin and tilted my head up.

My eyes widened when I noticed the fake sprig of mistletoe directly above us.

"You wanna?" he asked.

"Yeah, I do."

When his lips touched mine, it felt like fire and ice devouring me. And when he deepened the kiss, I felt myself falling down a rabbit hole I prayed would never, ever stop.

After what only felt like a moment, but must have been a lot longer, I heard the faint noise of our parents screaming in delight.

"It's about time," my mom had said.

I pulled back and buried my face in Corbin's chest.

"I thought you two would never get together," Mrs. Deeks said.

I could feel the heat burning up my neck and into my face.

"So, when's the wedding?" my father and Mr. Deeks both asked in unison.

The End

Author's Notes

So, what did you think about my first Rom-com?

This was an idea I had back in January of 2021, right as I was recovering from having Covid. I missed Christmas with my family. In fact, most everyone missed it due to Covid. I lived in Southern California at the time and the rate of infection was seriously high. Hardly anyone was out and about by the middle of December thanks to having it, or being exposed to it. So, when January came around, I drove up to Washington state to see my parents, my sister, and her family. Normally, I would have been with them over Christmas in December.

Nothing was the same. My sister had already taken down all of her decorations. Even though she told me she'd keep her fake tree up, she didn't. We had our gifts sitting on the ground in the living room next to the sofa, no tree in sight. They had all already done their gift exchanges so the majority of the gifts were for me. I had brought gifts for all of them, but since I had the most presents, it was weird.

No hot apple cider

No funny Christmas sweaters

No Christmas movies

No mistletoe

We didn't even have a turkey dinner, or anything normal. While I was happy to see my family, especially my niece and nephew, it felt more like a winter visit than a Christmas visit. The worst part, no snow. Usually, when I visit at Christmas there is snow, but there wasn't this year. It wasn't even that cold.

So, as I drove home, this idea hit me. What if the entire world decided to celebrate Christmas in July?

I wrote my notes down in January and put them aside. But the story continued to hound me. Once I finished up the Triple J Ranch series, I decided to write this book. It is a standalone, so no need to worry if there will be a series to keep up with. However, if I see there's enough people leaving reviews wanting more, I do have an idea for Corbin and Millie's wedding. But, if you want to see Wedding Crazy in June, then you'll have to make sure to leave a review on this book and tell me you want it.

What's next on my agenda to write? Three Christmas books! LOL From October 2021 to November 2021 I will launch 3 books. 2 of which will be in the Big Sky Christmas series (books 1-2 are already live and book 3 is on pre-order). Then I'll start a new series under my other pen name, J.L. Hendricks. This new series is about misfits in supernatural packs and communities. It's a spin-off from the Miss Claus series that was about Santa and his daughters. This new one is called Misfit Island and it's all about how misfits from the supernatural community find a new home and new family. Sadly, not everyone is happy about the island down at the end of the world. And eventually, Santa will hear about it, too. Although, he's going to have a different take on it than most think he will. There will be one book a year released at Christmas time until it's completed.

I really hope you and your family are able to enjoy Christmas this year, no matter how you celebrate it! I know I'm going to go all out. Maybe not Christmas Crazy, but there will be a much bigger celebration this year than normal.

And if you enjoyed Christmas Crazy in July, please be sure to tell your friends and family! And if you want to help others find this fun little gem, be sure to leave a review. Authors like me depend on readers to leave reviews. It helps others decide if it's something they want to read, or not.

And if you love Christmas books, then keep reading for a sneak peek at Her Montana Christmas Cowboy. A contemporary cowboy Christmas romance!

And if you join my newsletter, I'll send you a free book. And those on my newsletter will be the first to know what I release next, and when. Or you can follow me on and they will email you when I have a new release.

Newsletter Sign-up

By signing up for my newsletter, you will get a free copy of the prequel to the Triple J Ranch series, Finding Love in Montana. As well as another free book from J.L. Hendricks.

If you want to make sure you hear about the latest and greatest, sign up for my newsletter at: . I will only send out a few e-mails a month. I'll do cover reveals, snippets of new books, and giveaways or promos in the newsletter, some of which will only be available to newsletter subscribers. You'll also get a heads-up when I'm running sales on my books!

Sneak Peek

 Montana Christmas Cowboy

Chloe Manning's first Christmas in Frenchtown was heartbreaking. Will Santa give her her heart's desire during her second?

Brandon Beck left behind a woman for the benefit of his family ranch last Christmas. Now that he's back, why can't he get her out of his heart and mind?

When Santa and Mrs. Claus play matchmaker, will Chloe and Brandon fall under their Christmas Magic? Or will past hurts and fears keep them apart?

Don't miss out on the first Christmas story of the heart-warming Christmas Cowboy romance series, Big Sky Christmas. Where the romance is clean, and Christmas takes center stage!

Prologue

"Oh!" Chloe Manning yelled as her foot slipped where the driveway met wet grass. The water pooling on the concrete driveway wasn't something she'd planned on when scheduling her move. Since it had rained early that morning, she could not have foreseen the hazard and rescheduled. But, she also knew that her brothers and sister had scheduled their week to help on this one day. "Great, just what I ne—"

A strong, masculine hand reached down and offered to help her up.

"Thanks," she said without looking up.

"My pleasure." A husky voice that Chloe didn't recognize turned her face up just as she stood, and she yanked her hand out of his. "Ah!" Not looking where she was going, Chloe fell over the headboard she had dropped when she'd fallen the first time. This time she fell on the wooden headboard and smacked her knee good.

"I'm sorry, I shouldn't have let go until you were steady." The stranger furrowed his brow and bent down to help her get back up, again.

"No, no. It was all my fault." Chloe's face heated up, and she did her best to stand. She inhaled a quick breath when she put pressure on her right leg. While she knew enough medicine to know she hadn't broken anything, she was going to be sore.

In addition, she'd fallen flat on her face not once, but twice, in front of a very handsome cowboy. Her pride had also taken a huge hit. To make matters worse, Chloe hadn't dressed to impress; she was wearing an oversized, faded University of Montana sweatshirt and yoga pants. Her blonde hair was up in a messy ponytail, and she had zero makeup on. The only upside was that she doubted this handsome cowboy would recognize her again.

A bright, white smile greeted her when she stopped wobbling and took a step away from him. "Thank you. I don't know what's gotten into me today."

"Are you the one moving in?" The cowboy looked between her and the house.

Chloe nodded. "Yup."

"Well, welcome to Frenchtown. You must be the new medical billing manager everyone has been talking about." The cute cowboy put his hand out. "I'm Brandon Beck."

Well, there went that thought. He knew exactly who she was. No way was she going to be able to hide her embarrassment behind anonymity.

Standing taller, she straightened her sweatshirt and blew her bangs out of her eyes. When she took his hand, a jolt of electricity swept through her entire being. "Ah, I'm..." She cleared her throat. "I'm Chloe Manning." She shook his hand and noted the calluses, but also the strength in his warm touch.

"Nice to meet you, Miss Manning." When he ended the handshake, he touched the brim of his hat and nodded.

"This is my sister, Elizabeth, and our brothers." Chloe pointed to them all and introduced her five brothers to Brandon.

Elizabeth looked between Chloe and Brandon and gave her twin sister a sly smile. If Elizabeth didn't know better, she'd think Chloe already had an admirer. But really, who *wouldn't* be attracted to Chloe, even in moving clothes? The men of Beacon Creek had always admired her sister. The only reason Chloe wasn't already married was because she had made it known far and wide that she wanted to move away as soon as possible.

Brandon took a closer look at the newest resident to Frenchtown, and something in his gut told him to watch out for this little filly. She just might cause *him* to fall at *her* feet. He wondered if that would be so bad.

Once Brandon had moved on, the sisters went inside with the headboard and set it up in Chloe's new bedroom.

"Wow, sis. You did good. This is a rental?" Elizabeth Manning walked around the room checking out the wooden floor and blocked wainscoting on all the walls. "There's so much potential with this place."

Chloe Manning agreed. She couldn't wait until the day the owners let her buy it. This was exactly what she wanted. The deal she'd made was to rent for a year, and if everyone was happy then she would buy it. The owners wanted to make sure she stayed there with her job and didn't go home. Mr. and Mrs. Rice, who owned the quaint house, lived next door and felt it was important to like their neighbors. They worried if they sold her the house now, she would leave and sell to someone they may not like.

Chloe knew she was home and wouldn't be going anywhere. "Yes, I think I'm going to be very happy in this house, and in this town." She beamed at her sister as they unloaded their boxes into a spare room.

Chloe and Elizabeth were twins. While Chloe had always wanted to get out of Beacon Creek, Elizabeth was happy to live there for the rest of her life. When Chloe was offered the chance to move to Frenchtown and manage the local medical clinic's administrative side, she'd jumped at the chance to leave her small hometown. Not that Frenchtown was much bigger, but it did offer her a chance at new experiences and a promotion at work.

The plan was to work in the Frenchtown Clinic and manage it for the next five to seven years, and then she could start applying for jobs in the big cities, like Bozeman or Helena. Then, she would be doing exactly what she had wanted her entire life—get out of Dodge, so to speak.

"What about the men? If they're all as handsome as that cowboy we just met, then I think I won't be the only one getting married next year," Elizabeth teased her sister.

Heat shot up Chloe's neck and face. She deserved the ribbing after everything she'd put Elizabeth through when her now fiancé came back to town last summer.

The man who had helped Chloe up from the ground was gorgeous. Too bad he'd met her when she was at her worst. No makeup, hair a mess, and then to fall flat on her backside? She knew he wouldn't be back.

Just thinking about slipping and falling in front of the handsome Brandon Beck caused her face to heat up again. She wasn't normally a klutz, but today seemed to be her day of making a fool out of herself.

Even after he'd helped her up, she'd still tripped over the headboard because she wasn't looking where she was going. Instead, she was focused on the very good-looking and tall cowboy with chocolate-brown eyes and medium-brown hair that looked as though it needed a cut. His hair curled around his ears and above the back of his collar, which only served to make Chloe even more attracted to the cowboy.

All she could think of was running her fingers through his soft hair. Where that thought came from, she couldn't say. But when she'd realized where her mind was, that was when she'd tripped over the headboard.

―――――――――

Does this sound like fun? If you enjoy reading about the faith and fun surrounding a small town at Christmas, then this book is for you! And it can be enjoyed year-round. So, check out today! You'll be glad you did.